The
Friends
of the
Loony Lake
Monster

Other books by Frank Bonham

The
Friends
of the
Loony Lake
Monster

FRANK BONHAM

E. P. Dutton & Co., Inc.   New York

Published simultaneously in Canada by Clarke, Irwin & Company Limited, Toronto and Vancouver

SBN: 0-525-30205-0   LCC: 72-78091

Designed by Dorothea von Elbe
Printed in the U.S.A.
First Edition

To Marci,
and her Little Women:
Christy, Wendy, Jill
With love

1

GUSSIE GRANT arrived in Oregon on a night of wild wind and pelting rain. She lay across the seat of a rented moving van with her head on her mother's lap. She was neither asleep nor awake. She and her parents had been driving for two days, and the steady snore of truck tires had put her into a trance.

But now, suddenly, her father turned off the engine. Gussie tried to open her eyes, but they remained tightly closed, as though her eyelids had been sewn shut. The rain hissed on the truck's metal roof, and the wind moaned. In a moment her father would roll down the window, a man would say, "Fill her up?" and Mr. Grant would say, "Yes."

But he didn't. He said, "Well, here we are!"

And her mother said, "That *rain*! It's coming down in *buckets*!"

"Well, your uncle always said there was no guessing about the weather up here. Either it rains or it doesn't."

Gussie's mother shivered and said, "Why don't you run up the periscope, and we'll see what it's doing now?"

Gussie smiled to herself. One pants leg had twisted up and her ankle was chilled. She was slowly coming out of her trance, like bubbles rising in a jar of honey. She knew they had arrived at Fern Hill Ranch, where they were going to live, and she understood everything her parents were saying. But she could not move.

Then she heard her father say, "You and Gussie may as well wait here while I go inside and start a fire. Got the keys?"

There was a pause. The rain splattered against the truck.

"The keys?" said Gussie's mother. "No, don't you remember? I gave them to you just before we left."

"You gave them to me?" said Mr. Grant. "Not that I remember."

"I put them on the kitchen windowsill five minutes before we left, and I said, 'Here are the keys. You'd better put them in your pocket right now.'"

"Yes, dear, but *I* said, 'Uncle Fred was *your* uncle, and it's *your* ranch now, so *you* keep them.' Remember?"

"No," said Gussie's mother. "Because I was trying to decide where to put Gussie's French horn, with the van already full—"

"Great!" said Gussie's father. "Know where the keys are, Fern? On a windowsill a thousand miles from here! Excuse me—I'll just trot back and get them."

The rain swished and splattered and blew against the windows. There was a hollow moaning of wind. Gussie felt as though she should be helping, somehow. But she was numb. She lay limp and half-asleep. Memories of the life they had left circled around her like fish in a dark pool. She remembered the things her mother used to say to her.

Don't run, Gussie! The people downstairs will complain. If you're going to practice your French horn, you'll have to go down to the laundry room. I don't know why you don't give up on that big old horn and take ballet lessons, like other girls.

Because my feet are too big. Why doesn't she play baseball, like I do? Why can't I have a dog?

Because there's no room for a dog in the apartment.

Then why don't we move to the country?

Because your daddy is an advertising man, and this is a very nice apartment, and it's close to his work.

Well, I wish he were a sheep rancher, like Uncle Fred. This apartment is so small I'll probably grow up to be a midget.

Well, he's not, and if you want to raise sheep I guess you'll have to marry a rancher.

I'm only nine, Mother. Don't be silly.

And then the telegram had come saying that Uncle Fred had died in a tractor accident, at the age of seventy-

3

six, and he had left the ranch to Gussie's mother, his only living relative.

Gussie's father quit his job, bought a lot of books and magazines on raising sheep, and borrowed all the money he could. Uncle Fred had left them the ranch, but no money. He had a thousand acres of land, and twenty-seven dollars in the bank.

Mr. Grant drove the car up to the ranch, near Agate City, Oregon, and locked it in the garage. An old man named Percy was keeping an eye on the ranch. Then Mr. Grant came home on the bus, rented a moving van, loaded everything they owned into it, and off they went.

And now they were here, but they were going to have to sleep in the car.

"Know what?" said her father, suddenly. "I'll bet Percy's got a key hidden somewhere on the porch."

The truck door squalled open and a draft of cold air blew against Gussie's face. The raw, damp chill of it succeeded in waking her. She licked her dry lips and gazed up at the dome light. The door slammed and the light went off. Gussie raised her head.

"Awake?" her mother asked.

"Uh-huh. Are we there?"

"Yes, but we can't go in yet. Why don't you—"

Gussie sat up. Through the rain slithering down the windshield, she saw her father step onto the porch in his wet windbreaker. The house was an old, dark, two-story building with a peaked roof and small windows.

Standing there in the black and rainy night, it looked like a haunted house. Gussie yawned, stretched, and suddenly slid under the wheel to get out of the car. Her mother said she was like a cat: a good yawn and a stretch and she was always ready to go.

She pushed the door open and yelled: "Wait for me, Daddy! I know how we can get in—"

2

THE HOUSE, a tractor, and a lot of rusty farm equipment lay in the greenish twilight of a lamp on a power pole. They had stayed here several times on vacations. Gussie remembered how the house was braced against the hillside. There was a pasture below it where an old horse named Frisky had been retired. And there were gnarled fruit orchards, a couple of rickety barns, and a dark fir woods between the house and the highway above it.

They had never stayed long when they visited, because the house had a funny smell and was littered with junk. And her uncle was always busy. He was a nice old man, but he insisted on making a custard for them that was soupy, with flecks of soot in it from the stove. It tasted like cold fried egg.

"Break a window!" Gussie told her father grimly,

shivering with the cold. "I'll crawl inside and unlock the door." She began jumping up and down on the porch to keep warm. The boards sprang under her like a diving board.

Her father looked under a muddy gunnysack that lay as a doormat, then ran his finger along the lintel above the door. "I've got a feeling Percy has a key hidden here somewhere—"

But finally he gave up hope of finding the key. He picked up a piece of firewood from a stack near the porch. He told Gussie to stand back. Then he smashed the porch window. As he was breaking off the sharp daggers of glass around the frame, the lights of a car swept down the S curve of the road to the house.

"POLICE!" Gussie hissed. "They heard you break the window, and they're coming to investigate!" She flattened her back against the door and faced the oncoming lights.

"Relax, supergirl," her father said. "It's probably Percy. He's seen our lights. Another nice thing about living in the country is that *real* things will happen, so you won't have to use your imagination so much."

Its tires squishing in the mud, a pickup truck stopped near the little van and a man in a yellow raincoat got out. A medium-sized dog jumped out with him. The man wore a dust-colored rancher's hat. He took it off to say hello to Gussie's mother, in the truck, and Gussie could see the rain dancing on his bald head. He stood there muttering bashfully to her, then put on his hat and came on to the house.

7

"Percy?" Gussie's father called.

"That's me. Saw your lights when you drove in, and come over to say hello."

He was an old man with a long face and squinting eyes, and he looked rather like a horse. Gussie knew he was a sheep rancher who lived a mile or so away. He winked at Gussie. The dog stood wiggling all over and seemed to grin at her. It was able to bare its front teeth.

"What's your dog's name?" she said.

"Al," Percy said. "What's yours?"

"Gussie."

"Did you break that window, Gussie? It was all right when I checked this morning."

"*He* did it," Gussie said, pointing at her father.

Gussie's father sighed. "Percy," he said, "did you know that half the men in prison are there because some woman told them to do something? Well, as long as it's broken, Gussie," he said, "you might as well go inside and let us in."

The icy air of the old house closed on Gussie like a trap. Her teeth began to chatter as she let the others in. "I'll get a fire started right away," Percy said.

Gussie sniffed the air. The place smelled like a combination of wet wool, bacon grease, and a wet campfire. It was even messier than the last time Gussie had seen it, two years ago. A ham hung from a ceiling hook in one corner. There was a pile of dirty sheep fleeces beneath the ham. Near the fireplace, someone had dumped a dozen muddy chunks of firewood. In front of the sofa she saw an anvil. She knelt, picked up a hammer lying near it, and began to strike the anvil. It made a sharp, ringing sound. The dog, Al, began to moan, softly and apologetically. Gussie stopped pounding. It was hurting her ears, too.

"What's the anvil doing in the house?" she asked Percy.

Water was sliding off Percy's yellow raincoat and puddling on the floor as he lit the fire. "I think your uncle brought it in last winter to work on some harness."

Gussie squinted at the flames beginning to leak up through the chunks of oak in the fireplace. "Percy?" she said, frowning.

"That's me."

"What?"

"You said 'Percy,' and I said, 'That's me.' "

"Oh. . . . Percy, what happened to Uncle Fred?"

"Tractor turned over on him."

Gussie pretended to retch. Her parents had not told her about that, though she had suspected something of the sort. "How could it?"

"He tried to turn it on a steep hillside. That's always dangerous. Although—"

Percy sat on a chopping block near the sofa and tested his raspy whisker-stubble with his fingertips, as if making sure his jaw was still there.

"Although what?" said Mr. Grant, who came in just then carrying some suitcases.

"Nothing, Tom," Percy said mysteriously. "I made your beds yesterday. Better turn the covers back so

9

they'll warm up a little. This fireplace is the only heat, except for some coal-oil heaters. Been pretty nippy, for May. Late rains, too. This'n may be the last."

Gussie's father went into the bedroom, off the living room. Sitting on the anvil, Gussie lowered her voice.

"Although what, Percy?"

Al was licking the puddles that had formed on the rug around Percy. The fire was not drawing well. Smoke was pouring out into the room. Gussie wondered whether that was all right. She had never seen the fireplace smoke like that before.

Percy squinted at her. "Do you believe in monsters?" he whispered.

"Yes!" Gussie believed in anything exciting. There were whales and elephants. Why not monsters? "Did a monster kill him?" she asked, awed.

Percy tightened his lips. "Tell you sometime," he said.

Gussie hit the toe of the anvil with the hammer. It sounded muted, and she could feel it vibrating in her bones. "Percy?" she asked thoughtfully.

"That's me."

"Is the smoke supposed to come out like that?"

Thick and white, a sweet-smelling smoke was rapidly filling the upper half of the room. The old man twisted on the chopping block.

"Holy cow, no! I forgot to open the damper."

His arm vanished into the smoke. There was a squeal of rusty iron, and the smoke was sucked up the chimney as the flames leaped. "Son of a gun," said Percy.

Gussie grinned and reached out a hand to Al, trying to coax him to her. Al got up politely, but Percy pulled him back.

"Nope," he said. "Al's a working dog, missy—very fine Australian Kelpie. Got teeth like razors, and a mind like Einstein. You can't play with Kelpies, or they forget they're hired men. Sit down, Al, you lovely thing."

Al, whose coat was matted with burrs and mud, grinned with his front teeth and sat down. Gussie grinned back with her front teeth, and her lips silently framed the words, *Good dog!* She knew he knew she liked him.

Mrs. Grant came from the kitchen, still wearing her sweater, with a scarf over her head. She looked slightly dazed, as though somebody had been spinning her in a swing. She had not been quite so anxious to become a rancher's wife as Gussie's father had been to become a rancher. Gussie guessed it would be different, without a shopping center a block away and servicemen nearby to repair the television set. In fact, there *was* no television set here.

"Come on in and have a hot drink, everybody," she said. And she took a breath and wearily blew out her cheeks.

3

THEY GATHERED at the table in the kitchen. A wood vise was nailed to one corner of it and the top was covered with threadbare oilcloth. Steaming cups of coffee and a mug of hot chocolate rested on the faded rose pattern. Gussie warmed herself before the rusty wood-burning stove. She turned her face back and forth as though it were a marshmallow she was roasting. Rain spattered against the window like handfuls of bird shot. She sat down and sniffed the steam of her hot chocolate.

"So you're going to be a sheepman," said Percy, spooning lumpy sugar into his coffee.

"I'd better be, Percy," said Mr. Grant, grimly. "Two more weeks in that ad agency and I'd have jumped out the window. I've been reading all the stuff I could find on sheep-ranching, but I'll need a lot of advice. And on top of not knowing the business, I'm broke."

"Can't you borrow money on the ranch?"

"Uncle Fred already thought of that. When he died, the ranch had more loans on it than a mile of used cars. So it's going to be close. But we'll make it."

He smiled uncertainly.

"Sure you'll make it," said Percy. He started telling Mr. Grant about ways to cut corners, but Gussie's mind wandered back to the monster he had hinted at. She leaned toward her mother.

"Fern," she whispered. She liked her mother, and usually called people she liked by their first names. "Uncle Fred was killed by a monster!"

Everyone had stopped talking when she started whispering, and her voice carried like a shout. They all looked startled, even Al, whose ears came to attention. Gussie put her hand over her mouth.

Percy seemed upset. His long horse-face saddened. "I didn't *say* that, Gussie! All's I said—" He broke off and dug at a broken thumbnail that looked as if it were made out of wood. "There's some custard in the refrigerator," he muttered. "Fred made it some time back. May still be good."

Yecch, thought Gussie.

"Percy," Gussie's mother sighed, "let me tell you something about children. If you tell them monster stories at night, they usually wake up screaming. But

13

since you've started, I think you'd better finish."

"I'm sorry, Fern. Didn't mean to start anything, but— Well, you know that little lake on your land—?"

Gussie's mother was laughing softly. "Loony Lake? On the Ryan homestead? Oh, yes! I used to visit there as a little girl. I know all about the monster. It lives in the lake, and once in a blue moon it comes out and makes footprints or something, and everyone starts whispering about *The Thing in the Lake!*"

Percy looked gratefully at her. "And that's all there is to it! Your uncle died when his tractor turned over on him. But some of the people who went out to bring the tractor in claimed they found the footprints of a monster near it, and they figured The Thing tipped the tractor over on him, or stepped on him, or— Well, you know how it goes."

"Yes, I know," said Fern Grant. "But I guess I've lived too long in the city to believe such tales. All footprints, and no monsters." She pulled off her scarf. The kitchen was growing warm, now.

"Where there's smoke, there's fire," Gussie said. She slurped some hot chocolate and looked at each of them.

A look of worry crossed her mother's face, but cleared as she said, with a gaiety Gussie knew was forced:

"I'll tell you what there *is*, though! A treasure!"

"Ryan's Treasure," Percy said, nodding.

"I dug holes all over the Douglas fir grove looking for it," Mrs. Grant said. "How much? Five thousand dollars?"

"At least."

Gussie drank her chocolate, refusing to be tempted from the monster story by a tale of treasure. *She could see it rising, dripping from the lake in the grove, its eyes glowing like a cat's as it dragged its terrible, scaly body through the trees toward the sound of Uncle Fred's tractor. It roared, but he couldn't hear it above the tractor sounds. Then—*

She shuddered.

Percy was telling about the treasure.

". . . A whole bag of gold pieces, the fella at the bank said! Ryan—he owned that little ranch your uncle bought after Ryan died, what we call the old Ryan place—it's yours, now—Ryan said he was going to San Francisco and get himself a wife and deck her out in diamonds and furs and bring her back."

Now it was getting interesting. Gussie thought of a beautiful lady in diamonds and furs coming to a homesteader's shack. What would she do when she learned there was no gas stove, and the toilet was in a little shack outside, with spiders under the wooden seat?

"Ryan was going to leave on Saturday, but when my father didn't see him leave by Monday, he rode over to cast an eye on things. Ryan was sitting bolt upright at the table. Dead as a doornail! But, you know what? *They never found a nickel of that gold!*"

He looked at Mr. Grant when he said it, patting his palms on the tabletop. Gussie hated to leave a live monster for a dead homesteader, but she asked quickly:

"Did they look under the floor?"

"Course! First place. And in the spring, in the oat

barrel and everywhere else. And, like your mother says, folks have dug lots of holes around there. Used to, don't any more. Fred put a stop to it. His animals kept stepping in them and getting hurt. Well, I'll leave you folks to get some sleep. Call me tomorrow, after you're up and around. I'll fill you in on things."

Percy spilled the rest of his coffee on the table as he got up. Gussie was afraid he would be embarrassed, but he just sloshed it away with the sleeve of his shirt. "Woops," he said.

Gussie's bedroom was up a crooked flight of stairs, and she would sleep there alone, the master bedroom being downstairs. Gussie's little room was chilly and damp. It had one window and a peaked ceiling, like a tent. Her parents tucked her in and said they would leave the hall light burning. Now that it was time for the lights to go out, the monster story rose up with its green eyes burning. . . .

She asked her mother some more questions about Ryan's Treasure, but while her mother talked soothingly, unbraiding her hair, she was wondering whether it was a long-necked, meat-eating one that could stick its head in upstairs windows and pluck children out of their beds like chocolates out of crinkled paper nests. . . .

There was a stain on the ceiling shaped like a lizard. *Was* it a lizard? Her gaze kept coming back to it uneasily. At last she thought of something.

"Daddy? Will you get my French horn out of the truck? It isn't raining now."

"What for?"

"Somebody might steal it."

Mr. Grant wasn't anxious to get it, but he did. He returned, puffing, and set it in the corner. Then they left her alone. Gussie got up. The horn was in a large black case shaped like a garden snail. The French horn was too big for her, but she wanted to be ready to play in the band when she reached junior high school. Her mother had tried to interest her in a little instrument called a piccolo, but she had only laughed.

"It looks like a leaky soda straw," she had said.

She opened the window and shivered in the glacial wind that blew her nightgown against her body. She wet her lips, filled her lungs, and practiced the fingering of the tune she had decided to play the first night at Fern Hill, like a bugler letting the enemy know the cavalry had arrived. The tune was the first seven notes of Haydn's *Surprise Symphony*.

She started blowing. The strong, honking notes of the horn rang out over the hilly range, across the rolling, dark sheep pastures and fir woods. *Da-da, dee-dee, DA-DA, da!* they sang.

Then she lowered the horn. In their little apartment in Los Angeles, people would have been pounding on the walls by now. Then a sound floated through the open window, a wild, moaning call from the direction of Loony Lake. Gussie gasped. An echo? It didn't sound like one. Cattle? Maybe.

What it really sounded like was a wild animal.

She put the horn away and hurried to slide under

the covers. Her electric blanket was not unpacked yet, and with all the heavy woolen blankets of Uncle Fred's on top of her, it was like being on the bottom in a wrestling match.

Then she had to get up again to close the window. Vexed, she crawled back in bed, muttering to herself.

Percy was a nice old man, but he should know better than to tell monster stories at night. Anybody should know better than that.

4

THE NEXT MORNING the Grants were up at daybreak. Mrs. Grant was going to take Gussie to Agate City to enroll her in school, although there were only three weeks left before summer vacation. Gussie hated having to leave the ranch and go to school at a time like this. The rain had blown away, and the sun had heated the barn and sheds so that they, and the tops of the fence posts, steamed like tea kettles. The sky was a clear blue. Her father and Percy would start unloading the truck today, and she would miss all that.

When it came time to leave, Gussie brought her French horn and catcher's mitt to the car. "You aren't taking those, are you, dear?" her mother said.

"Yes. I'll explain about them at News Time."

"Some schools don't have News Time."

"May I have the key? I'll put the horn in the trunk."

The important thing, Gussie knew from experience, was not to enter a new school like a kindergartner. They would start squeezing her into shape immediately, like a piece of putty. But she already had a shape that she liked, and she would have to let them know about it.

Mrs. Grant put the horn in the back seat. She tried to forget the catcher's mitt, but Gussie placed it on top of the horn case. As they drove out, she saw Percy on a hillside near the road, trying to start a big yellow tractor. Al sat on the seat beside him.

My gosh! Gussie thought. I hope it doesn't turn over on him! She leaned out the window, braids flying, to yell and wave at him, and he waved back.

On the way to Agate City, they passed a couple of lumber mills where big smokestacks like upside-down tea strainers fumed out thick, yellowish smoke. Then they came from their road, Old 101, Percy had called it, onto Pacific Highway, and saw the ocean. A few miles south they came to the town of Agate City, lying damp and green under a gray mattress of fog. The school was on a cliff above the ocean.

Mr. Myers, the principal, told them he had heard about their coming to the sheep ranch. "I'm going to put Augusta in Miss Baker's fourth-and-fifth combination," he said. "Room 20."

What about me? thought Gussie. Then she remembered that she *was* Augusta. It had been the name of Uncle Fred's wife, too.

Gussie's mother smiled reassuringly as Gussie walked away carrying her horn case, catcher's mitt, and lunch box. It was five minutes before schooltime, and children skipped and played about the grounds. Before some of the rooms, a handful of kids were waiting for the bell to ring. The school was only one story high, and each classroom opened on the playground. At Room 19, six or seven children watched her as she came by.

A red-faced boy jumped in front of her. "What's in the case?" he asked her.

"A man-eating snail," Gussie said, with a grin.

The boy followed her to Room 20, where a double line of boys and girls waited in perfect order. It was the only room where anyone was lined up.

"Let's see it eat your lunch!" the boy yelled, pawing at the case and her lunch box.

Gussie pulled away, the boy still trying to get the case open. Suddenly a tall boy before Room 20 said sharply:

"Arthur! Knock that off."

Arthur turned away sheepishly and slunk back to Room 19. Gussie smiled at the tall boy. She was going to say, jokingly, that she'd have fed the boy to her snail if he had kept it up. But then she saw that this boy was frowning, and that he was apparently in charge of the boys and girls standing in line. Despite the cold morning, he wore short sleeves. His hair was cut very short, like that of a World War II Marine, and he stood straight, with his hands at his sides.

Then she saw something that startled her: On his

left forearm the letters MOTHE were crookedly tattooed in blue! That T was too high, and the word did not spell anything that Gussie knew.

"Are you Augusta Grant?" the boy said.

"Yes," Gussie said. "They call me Gussie. I'm looking for—"

"Room 20, Miss Baker's room. I'm Tex Fuller. I heard you were coming. Fall in behind the last person in the girls' line."

Why should I? Gussie thought. But the boy had an air of command, like the principal, and she took her place at the end of the girls' line. There were a lot more girls than boys, she noticed.

None of the kids whispered or moved. Gussie leaned out to see what Tex was doing now, and found herself looking into his cold blue eyes. He made a hand gesture which said, *Move back in line!* Gussie did so.

Boy, this kid is too much, she thought. Still, he had taken her side. She hoped he was merely one of those firm-but-fair people, not really a mean one.

The bell jangled. Up and down the building, other kids went piling helter-skelter into class. But at Room 20, no one moved until Tex Fuller said:

"Girls' line! Forward—MARCH!"

The girls marched primly into the room and took their seats. Gussie, having no seat, stood near the teacher's desk. Then the boys came shuffling in. Tex told her to take an empty place near him.

Two minutes later, a pretty little blonde teacher

hurried in carrying books, keys, and a whistle. "I'm sorry to be late, children," she said breathlessly, "but I had to pick up the slip on our new girl, Augusta Grant."

Tex raised his arm. Miss Baker, looking rather timid, said, "Yes, Tex?" She was very young, like the practice teachers they had had once in a while in Los Angeles.

"She calls herself, Gussie, Miss Baker. Don't forget the flag salute."

Miss Baker asked Tex to lead the salute to the flag.

Then she made a little talk about the new girl, while Gussie squirmed. "Her parents own the old Hill place, now, and they'll be ranching there. Gussie, would you like to come up and tell us about yourself, and perhaps let us see what's in the big case?"

Gussie marched up. She was scared by all the faces, and started talking fast. She told them how old she was, and where she came from, and then she took the horn out of the case.

"I won't play it now," she said, "but if there's a school band maybe I will there, and this is my catcher's mitt, and I would have played catcher on the Little League team, only they wouldn't let girls play."

Tex appeared keenly interested in what she had said about the mitt.

Just before the first recess, Miss Baker caught a girl passing a note to a friend. "Cindy," she said, "would you like to read us what you think is more interesting than number sets?"

The girl immediately began to sob. No threat nor urging would make her read it.

"Tex," said Miss Baker, "will you take the letter from Cindy and read it to us?"

Tex took the crumpled slip of paper and read aloud,

" 'Gussie's uncle was killed by the L __ K E M __ __ S T E R. I wouldn't live out there for anything!' "

With a turn of the lip, Tex handed the note back to Cindy. "That's silly," he said. "There's no such thing as a lake monster."

The bell rang for recess. Tex marched them out.

5

TEX WAS good at arithmetic, but his reading was quite
poor. All the girls were better readers than the boys.
When the girls were asked to read a paragraph aloud,
they read it quickly and tried to rush on and read the
next. The boys frowned and scratched their heads and
muttered along. Tex got stuck on "cantaloupe," and
although Gussie had never read it before, she was able
to sound it out, so she raised her arm and Miss Baker
called on her.

"Can-ta-loupe," Gussie said. "Just like it's spelled,
only you don't pronounce the 'u.'"

Without looking up, Tex repeated the word and
continued to read, scowling. Gussie saw kids staring at
her and exchanging shocked glances. *Oh, boy, she's
gonna get it!* their faces said. She knew then that it was

probably considered dangerous to make Tex look bad by doing something he could not. Too late now.

When the bell rang for lunch, the kids did not stampede from Room 20 as Gussie heard the students of other rooms doing. Gussie saw the hungry children trembling like puppies eager to rush from the house for a romp. But they waited, while Tex cleared his desk, rather fussily, it seemed to Gussie. Then he said:

"Now hear this: File out. No shoving or socking."

Gussie was about to get up and leave when Tex spoke to her across the aisle. "I want to see you after class."

Gussie opened her mouth to say, *Who do you think you are?* Then she looked at the little blonde teacher, who gave her a sympathetic smile, and a shrug, but got up quickly and left.

Is this nut going to try to spank me or something? Gussie wondered. *Because I read the word?*

When they were alone, Tex said, "Can you catch with that mitt, or do you just carry it around?"

"I catch with it. I was better than Buzz Barton, but he got to catch for Andy's Body Shop, in Little League, just because he was a boy."

"Put on the mitt and stand in that corner, near the ant farm. I'm going to burn a couple over and see if you can really catch."

Gussie pulled on the mitt, while Tex took a ball from his desk, placed himself across the room from Gussie, and warmed up. "I'm pitcher on the school team," he said. "But my catcher is lousy."

"You won't be pitcher long if you throw a curve

through one of these windows," Gussie said, crouching down with the mitt before her.

Tex did not even answer that. He finished warming up, then stood straight, the back of his left hand on his hip as he faced her. Then his body convulsed and he let go a fast pitch.

Smack!

Right in the middle of her glove. Gussie smiled coolly and tossed the ball back. She flipped her left braid back over her shoulder. Tex threw three more, all of which she caught.

"Now, this next one is going to break to your left. Be ready for it."

Gussie picked it off just before it could pass through a window. Tex nodded.

"Okay," he said. "You caught me pretty well. Do you want to play four-square with the girls, or baseball with us?"

"Baseball, of course," Gussie said.

"We choose up sides after lunch, at 12:20. Be there on time if you want to play. There's a big shortage of boys in our school. It's too late in the season for you to play on the school team, but I think you might shape up pretty well next year."

"Thank you," Gussie said. Tex was strange, but she could not help liking him. He had not even added that she was good "for a girl."

Fifteen minutes before the last bell rang, a monitor brought a note from Mr. Myers' office. The monitor was a yellow-haired boy who stood there scraping his hair out of his eyes and snuffling. "Thank you, John," Miss Baker said.

"Will Gussie and Tex please stay after class for a moment?" she added.

Tex marched the kids from the room, dismissed them, and returned. Miss Baker said:

"Your mother telephoned, Gussie. Your father had to take his tractor to Tex's father's garage for some welding, and you're to meet him there."

Gussie looked at Tex, and shrugged. "Okay. Can I leave my horn here?"

" 'May I,' not 'can I.' Yes, you may."

The crossing guards were still on duty when they left the school. One of them lunged from the curb with his long red STOP sign, and a boy on a bicycle had to halt. He pretended to be about to run the children down, until he recognized Tex. Then he smiled and called, "Hi, Tex."

They started down a street of small houses. Gussie had tied the sleeves of her sweater around her waist, so that it hung down behind her like an apron worn backwards. The houses were small, and there was moss growing between their shingles. Everything was still drenched from the rain.

"I was a crossing guard in Los Angeles," Gussie said.

"Well, it's too late to get you a job like that here," said Tex. "Besides, our guards are all boys."

"Why?"

Tex reached up and passed his hand back and forth over his crisp hair. "I don't know. I'll ask Mr. Myers sometime. I think I could get you on as girls' bathroom monitor."

Gussie wrinkled her nose. "What's *that*? Something to do with a toilet brush?"

"Bathroom monitors keep the kids from staying in the bathrooms and talking. The girl they've got now just stays in there during recesses and gabs with the girls she's supposed to keep moving. Any job," he added, "is what you make it. That's what my dad says."

A fog bank had rolled in from the sea, and the air was clammy with cold mist. Gussie's arms had goose bumps. "Wait a minute," she said. She stopped and pulled on her sweater. Tex crossed his arms as he waited. The blue letters tattooed on his left arm were displayed. Suddenly Gussie knew what MOTHE stood for.

"How do you spell 'mother'?" she asked, as they went on.

"*I* know. There's an R on it. I'm not that dumb. But my dad came in when I was doing it, and whaled me. He wouldn't even let me finish."

"Why did you do it?"

"Just did it. I did it with a pin and some ink."

"What did your mother say?" Gussie asked.

"Nothing. She died when I was eight."

"Oh. I'm sorry." Gussie plodded along, her head down.

"Then my father retired from the Navy and came home to stay with me. He was stationed on Guam.

Navy men are always being transferred. Sometimes my mother and I went with him when he got transferred, and sometimes we didn't. He was a chief machinist's mate. That's pretty good. He's got a tractor garage now, and he's the Government Hunter. He kills coyotes and bears for the ranchers when they get to raiding sheep herds. Know what I bet?" He grinned.

"What?"

"I'll bet Percy had something to do with your father's tractor breaking. That old guy's a menace. My dad says if there's a wrong way to do a thing, Percy'll find it. And if there isn't an old wrong way, he'll invent a new one."

He passed his hand over his bristly hair again, smiling faintly. He did not smile broadly, like most boys, with all his front teeth, but merely widened his mouth a little, like an adult who was not really listening when you told him something funny. Gussie noticed his tattoo again, and an idea went off in her head like a little firecracker. She knew what to do about MOTHER.

But she did not want to offend Tex, so she backed into the subject.

"You're a real good pitcher," she said.

"Thanks. You caught me a lot better than Wesley. Next year we'll go to work on Mr. Myers about a girl playing on the team."

"Thanks. I was noticing something. When you put your left hand on your hip, just before you pitch, your tattoo shows up very well."

Tex frowned. He did not answer. She hurried on.

"But it would be better if it spelled something. 'Mothe' is too long for 'moth,' and too short for 'Mother.' "

"I know. I thought maybe it would fade. I didn't really mean it to last forever, like my dad's tattoos."

Gussie tossed her mitt up, spinning, and caught it. "It probably will fade," she said. "But while you wait, it might as well spell something. I'll bet if you were to finish it now, your father would never notice. He's so used to it, he probably never even sees it."

Tex looked at the tattoo, then smacked it with his hand. "Hey, Grant, you got an idea there," he said. "I'll do it tonight!"

6

THEY TURNED down a side street toward the ocean. It was not paved, and was plowed with ruts where, in the late afternoon light, water gleamed like tin. Along the road grew occasional big, silent fir trees and some shrubs with waxy green leaves. Not far ahead stood a flatbed truck.

"That's Percy's truck," said Tex. "Guess he hauled your father's cat in for my dad to repair."

"What's a cat?"

"Caterpillar tractor. You've just got a little one, but it's big enough for the ranch work. I drive the cats on and off the trucks for my dad."

They came to Tex's mailbox. At the back of a clearing bordered by dark green trees stood a white house with a green tar-paper roof. A grimy garage stood near the house with a pile of rusting metal beside it. In front of the garage was a small yellow tractor. Gussie's father, Percy, and a man in a welder's helmet stood before it. Percy and Mr. Grant wore round black glasses. The man in the helmet held a torch with which he was repairing the yoke of the tractor. Red-hot sparks dripped from the blue-white core of the flame.

"Don't look at the flame!" Tex warned. "It'll blind you. I'll get us some glasses."

Standing near her father and Percy, Gussie pulled on the glasses Tex brought from the garage. Their lenses were green, and so dark that she could see little beside the white-hot flame of the welding torch, which made a hissing noise like an angry cat. After a moment, Tex's father said, "That'll do it."

He swung his mask up like the visor of a knight's helmet. It was held to his head by an elastic band. They all removed their glasses. Gussie watched Mr. Fuller take a pack of cigarettes from the pocket of his shirt and let one fall into his hand. After putting it between his lips, he touched the tiny torch flame to it. Then he switched off the torch and removed his mask. He put on a red baseball cap.

"Hello, skipper," he said to Gussie, with a grin. He was a big man in a blue work shirt, greasy jeans, and short black boots. Above his shirt pocket was a name tape that read: FULLER, RICHARD S.

"Hello," Gussie said.

"How about a drink?" Dick Fuller said. "Tex, run Mr. Grant's cat onto the truck. Then put away the torch and tanks."

Tex scrambled onto the tractor. He began squirting fumes from a spray can into an air intake.

"Well, maybe we can steal a minute for a cup of coffee," said Gussie's father. "But I've got to get back and unload my wife's piano from that one-way van. I'm paying rent on it until I turn it in."

"No problem, Tom," said Percy. "I'll give you a hand."

Dick Fuller laughed. "Don't let this old dum-dum go *near* your wife's piano, Grant! He'll drop his end of it, and that'll be the end of the symphony."

Gussie frowned at him indignantly. *He is not a dum-dum!* she wanted to say. But Percy only gave his squinty-eyed smile and explained bashfully:

"I nudged the corner of the Oregon National Bank with my grader once, and Dick's never let me forget it."

"*Nudged* it! I've seen house-wreckers work two days and do less damage than you did. They almost charged him with bank robbery."

Percy grinned, and glanced at the air to his left.

They went through a back porch into a kitchen. Dirty dishes were piled on the drainboard and there was a pan of food under a gray fur of mold. When Mr. Fuller opened the refrigerator, Gussie stared at what was inside it. It was entirely filled with cans of beer, except for one carton of milk!

34

Gussie poked her father's arm and pointed. Dick Fuller saw her do it.

"Quite a collection, eh, Gus? Doctor's orders. He told me to drink a lot of beer, after I had my ulcer operation."

"At least," Percy mumbled, "he told you not to drink whiskey."

"Same thing, Percy, same thing." Dick Fuller offered a can to Gussie's father.

"Not right now, thanks," Mr. Grant said. "Work to do."

Percy said he wouldn't have a beer either, and Mr. Fuller drank the can down without pausing for breath, then opened a second one. He drank this one too. Gussie heard the tractor start up with a sharp blatting sound. Mr. Fuller belched and patted his stomach.

"So you're going to make a million dollars in sheep," he said to Mr. Grant.

"I might settle for a little less than that," Gussie's father said. "The main thing is, we aren't cooped up in an apartment now, and I'm not having to write ads for Giovanni's Frozen Pizza and Zephyr Panty Hose."

"I'm glad you aren't planning on being a big shot," said Mr. Fuller, "because sheep are a losing proposition. Your wife's uncle would have gone broke in another year, if he hadn't died."

"Oh, it ain't that bad, Dick," said Percy.

"It ain't, huh? Listen, Grant, any of your lambs that don't freeze to death in a storm next winter, the eagles will carry off."

"No bout adout it, Dick, they do carry off a few," Percy agreed. "But what they're eating most of the time is varmints. Rats and rabbits and such. We *need* the eagles."

Fuller winked at Gussie's father. "Need them like Gus needs measles. Never shot an eagle, eh, Perc?"

"Maybe—before I knew better. Dr. Wigmore explained it all to me one time, about the balance of nature." He turned to Mr. Grant. "She was the high school biology teacher before she retired. Real smart woman. She's a bird watcher now."

"Bird *watcher!*" laughed Dick Fuller. "She's a *bird!* Gray-crested do-gooder. Wrote an article for the *National Geographic* on birdbaths! 'The West's leading expert on birdbaths,' they called her. Big deal. You listen to fools like Wigmore, Grant, and you'll be the West's leading expert on lamb losses. Look here—!"

He led them from the musty kitchen into a small, dark parlor with a tiny black fireplace like an Indian oven. From a rack he lifted a rifle. His hands fondled it and his eyes shone. The gun was the first clean thing in the house that Gussie had seen.

"This is my sweetheart," he said, in an affectionate growl. "Like to have a dollar for every eagle I've shot with this."

"They aren't *paying* a dollar an eagle these days, Dick," said Percy. "They're *fining* you if they catch you."

"Only if they catch you—and it's a big country. Well, anyway, when you start losing sheep, Grant, give

36

me a jingle. I'm the Government Hunter, you know. No charge."

"No, I didn't. Well, let's see if the boy's got the cat on the truck yet—"

But Fuller, his cigarette in his mouth, was sighting down the barrel of the rifle. "Know what I'd like to put a shot into?" he said, scowling.

Gussie looked out the window. Tex was driving the tractor up a steel ramp onto the back of the truck. No wonder he was a funny kind of a boy, she thought. He had a funny kind of a father. A dum-dum.

"What's that?" said Mr. Grant, coolly.

"That so-called lake monster of yours!"

Gussie looked around. "There's no such thing, is there?" she said.

"There's *something* over there in Loony Lake. I figure it's an alligator or a dolphin—"

"Alligators don't live in Oregon," said Percy, "and dolphins live in the ocean."

"Except fresh-water dolphins, Perc. Pranksters could have hauled one over to Loony Lake and dumped it in. So if you see anything funny over there, call me and I'll come over and kill it."

He replaced the rifle and stroked it fondly. "Yes sir, she's my baby. No sir, don't mean maybe," he added.

7

WHEN THEY reached the ranch, the sun was settling like a flattened orange into a pearly mist behind the ranch house. The fog would be thick on the coast tonight, said Percy, a real pea-souper. Gussie saw the van parked near the porch, empty except for her mother's spinet. Percy stopped the truck by an earthen ramp near a shed, then backed the tractor from the truck onto the ramp.

"There she is—as good as ever!" he said. "Now I'll take the truck back to my place and drive my little old bucket job over."

"What for?"

"Lift that piano off the truck and onto the porch slicker than popping peach pits at a porcupine! The bucket on it—that's the blade—is just the size of your little piano. Then you'll be able to drive the van to the U-drive place in the morning and not have to pay another day on it."

Percy drove off.

Gussie's mother had cookies and milk ready for her. All day, she said, she had been moving junk from the house into the barn. The pantry had been full of veterinary supplies—cans of black, evil-smelling sheep-dip; jars of screwworm ointment; dope to soften horses' hooves. An extra bedroom had been turned into a storeroom for scraps of broken harness and bags of wool. In the kitchen, she had opened a can of nutmeg for a pie and found it full of copper rivets.

Gussie ate, feeling tired. It had been a long day. Her mother sat down with a cup of coffee and patted her hand.

"Tell me about your new school," she suggested.

"It's okay, Fern. There's this boy, Tex, Dick Fuller's son. He's in my grade. He's got a tattoo."

She told about Tex's mother's dying, and Dick Fuller calling the rifle his sweetheart. "I don't like him much."

"Do you like Tex?"

"I haven't decided. If he's not too much like his father, I'll like him. But if he shows me a knife and says he kills rabbits with it and it's his sweetheart, that will be it for Tex!" She bared her teeth and drew her finger across her throat.

The hills were tiger-striped with shadow when Percy returned, driving a little rubber-tired tractor with a blade like a scoop in front. Al sat on the seat beside him.

Mr. Grant, pulling on gloves, looked doubtfully at the piano. "What's your idea, now, Percy?" he asked.

Percy lifted his dust-colored cowboy hat and adjusted it over one eye. "My idea is, I raise the bucket exactly to the level of the truck bed. Then you push the piano into the bucket. I swing the rig around and set the piano on the porch. After that, Gussie could practically roll it in the house herself."

He restarted the engine. Gussie and her mother stood on the porch, watching Percy push and pull the little ball-capped levers before him. The bucket could be raised and lowered, and tilted to dump its load. He ran the neat little tractor close to the back of the truck and climbed down to measure with his eye. Then he got up again and raised the scoop another inch. Now it was exactly level with the truck bed.

"Okay, Tom!" he told Mr. Grant. "Let her go!"

Mr. Grant carefully pushed the spinet into the bucket. It filled it snugly. Gussie held her breath, fearing that the piano might pull the tractor over on its nose. But Percy swung it nimbly and came toward the porch, as Gussie and her mother got out of the way. Mrs. Grant held both hands over her eyes.

I wish that smart-alecky Dick Fuller were here to see this, thought Gussie. *Percy's no dum-dum. He's a genius!*

Percy's hands searched and prodded among the levers. The bucket began to drop a little. Then the tractor seemed to snort and pick up speed. It was approaching the porch too fast! Percy made a couple of quick adjustments. The tractor stopped at the very edge of the porch railing. Suddenly the bucket began tipping forward as if to dump the piano out!

Gussie waved at Percy. "Percy, it's tipping!"

Percy's hands prodded and pulled. The tractor hummed to itself as the bucket tilted farther and farther forward. Gussie saw that Percy's long face was frozen into an expression of alarm. Al, seeming to know that something terrible was happening, leaned against Percy and bared his teeth. Then Percy grasped what he must have decided was the long-lost lever, for he gave it a yank and set himself back against the seat with a smile.

But the bucket jerked forward even faster! The piano began to roll on its little brass wheels. Without a pause it leaped neatly over the porch railing.

It landed face-down with a splintering crash. The walnut paneling split with an awful rending noise, like leg bones breaking. Glints of steel and brass showed through the wood, and there was an explosion of musical sounds as though the loudest piano sonata in the world had just ended.

And just when Gussie thought the long, jangling racket was over, a final string ripped loose with a throbbing twang. After that it was quiet. Al was standing up, panting. Gussie looked at her mother. Mrs. Grant's hands were still over her eyes. Finally she lowered them, and Gussie saw tears in her eyes. But she smiled bravely.

"Well, you got it on the porch, Percy," she said.

Percy squatted down and scratched Al's head. "Land o' Goshen!" he said. "I don't use that little rig much, and I guess I got the wrong lever. Just look at that."

Gussie felt worse for Percy than she did for the piano. He must feel terrible.

"Percy," Mr. Grant asked thoughtfully, "is there a good piano tuner in town?"

"No, there ain't, Tom," Percy said. And he sighed. "But I'll tell you what. I've got a perfectly good player piano at my place that I never use. It belonged to my mother. I'll take this, er, piano to the dump, and bring over my mother's old one. How'd that be, Fern?"

Mrs. Grant smiled again and nodded her head. "That would be lovely, Percy." Her lower lip trembled a little. Gussie knew she had adored the little spinet.

"I've got a lot of rolls of music for it, too. 'The Golden Eagle March,' and, 'It's a Long Way to Tipperary,' to name just two. Want to give me a hand with this, er, stuff, Tom?" Percy said.

As they began loading the remains of the spinet back into the bucket, Percy muttered sadly, shaking his head: "Just shows to go you."

8

GUSSIE HAD feared the old man would be so mortified by the piano accident that they would never see him again. The last they saw of him that evening was when, after dinner, he drove the tractor away into the night with the bucket full of piano parts, Al sitting disconsolately beside him. The dog looked back once, but Percy stared straight ahead.

But the next morning, as Mrs. Grant was doing Gussie's second braid in the downstairs bathroom, there came a knock at the door. "I'll get it, Fern!" Gussie said.

She opened the door, and it was Percy. He wore his cowboy hat, jeans, and boots, but no shirt—just long-sleeved underwear. His pickup truck was parked outside. Apparently he had been expecting Mr. Grant to open the door, because he looked right over Gussie's head, searching the room.

"Hi, Percy!" Gussie called up at him.

Percy looked down. "Oh—didn't see you down there. Where's your dad?"

Mr. Grant strolled in from the kitchen, holding a mug of coffee. "Got the piano tuned already?" He laughed, but Percy's face was tight with strain and excitement.

"HOGS!" Percy shouted.

Mr. Grant blinked. "Hogs? Is there a herd of wild hogs coming? Come in. We'll call the Government Hunter."

"Hogs on your Ryan place!" Percy blurted. He caught his toe on the anvil, and stumbled. Then he squatted down near the sofa, as Gussie had seen cowboys do in movies when they wanted to think.

"You've got four hundred acres over there around Loony Lake, Tom, at least a hundred of it in old orchards! The hogs would get fatter than ticks on the apples and pears that fell. It ought to support two hundred of them. Plus, there's acres and acres of tan-oak trees that ain't any use in the world but to drop acorns —and hogs love acorns. Hogs are a better cash crop than sheep, but most of this country ain't adapted to them."

Mr. Grant brought Percy a cup of coffee, and Percy sipped it, shivering with excitement. "That land's never been much good for raising anything but legends, but hogs would be a real money crop! It might get you out of the woods on your loans."

"What would I need?" asked Gussie's father. Gussie was now in the kitchen hastily eating breakfast, but she could hear them talking.

"Fencing—that's all! And a loading rig. The Ryan place is fenced, but it's been tore down in a few places. For a few hundred dollars worth of supplies, you could put it back in shape."

"What about labor? I've got to watch every nickel."

"I'm not busy right now. I'll get it started while you do what has to be done over here. Gussie could help on weekends. And Tex—he's a handy little kid. Probably be glad to pick up some money building fence. Get him out of the clutches of the Mighty Hunter too."

Mr. Grant decided hogs were worth a try. He asked Percy to make up a list of supplies they would need. As Gussie and her mother were hurrying out to the car to leave for school, he told Gussie that if she wanted to she could invite Tex out to work on the fence next weekend.

But something was wrong with Tex that day.

Gussie sensed it when he lined the boys and girls up before the bell rang. He was unusually severe with children who got out of line or talked. And his reading was even worse than usual.

Then, when the noon baseball game started, she was certain that he was sick, because his pitches were slow and erratic.

His left hand went up and rubbed his right shoulder. Gussie saw the tattoo on his arm—and gasped.

"You did it!" she whispered. "You put the R on MOTHER."

Tex nodded and began chewing his gum faster. "Yeah."

"Did—did he catch you?"

Tex glanced back at Arthur, as if to make sure he wasn't going to steal third. But Gussie knew he was just being sure nobody had moved in close enough to hear.

"No, but he saw it this morning. He whaled me," he said. "Couldn't make me cry, though."

Then, in a loud voice, he said: "Okay, you guys, that's the last floater I'm going to throw! You got to be glad I didn't feel like throwing my fast ball till now." He grinned wolfishly at the waiting batter.

Gussie returned to her position. She felt terrible. She had egged him on to the tattooing, and was completely responsible for his being whipped. Her state of mind was such that she let the next ball Tex threw get away from her, and Arthur stole home while she was tearing through a girls' four-square game after it.

It was a relief when the bell finally rang.

Tex lined the kids up before Room 20 so quickly that she had no chance to tell him about the fencing. He caught Wesley eating a marshmallow-filled cupcake, called a Jingle-Jangle, in line, and made him write on the blackboard, while they waited for Miss Baker:

46

"I will not eat Jingle-Jangles in line. I will not eat Jingle-Jangles in line." Except that Wesley spelled Jangles, "Jengles."

Tex sneered when he saw it. He made Wesley correct the misspelled words and do them another ten times. "He can eat them, but he can't spell them," he jeered.

Gussie realized that when Tex had a bad day, the whole class had one.

Miss Baker was a bit upset when she found Wesley, almost in tears, writing on the blackboard. She let him take his seat, and asked Tex:

"Why don't you let me handle discipline problems in this room, Tex?"

Tex smiled coolly. "Sure, Miss Baker. I hope we don't lose the Best Citizens flag, though, because this class was a rough one to handle, last fall. . . ."

The kids did a lot of whispering and note-passing during the next hour. Tex ignored all their mischief. Miss Baker's voice grew louder and louder and her hair became mussed. She tried separating the troublemakers and even resorted to tying a boy in his chair who was unable to keep from getting up and moving around. Gussie had only seen this done once before, and that was in second grade. The boy sat there grinning and making noises through his teeth.

Miss Baker tried to ignore the rising uproar, but finally, her blonde hair falling over her face and her eyes wild, she went to the door and said,

"I'm going to the supply room for a few minutes,

and when I come back I want you *all in your places,* and working on your number sets. Tex—I'll leave you in charge," she added.

After the door closed, Tex stood up and looked around the room. The children grew absolutely still. "Now hear this," he said. "All games and recesses will be canceled for the rest of the week if I hear another peep out of anybody."

The children smiled to themselves and happily got back to work.

After the last bell, Gussie asked Tex to carry her French horn for her. "I wanted to ask you something."

"Why not?" Tex said.

Gussie excitedly told him that her father would pay him to help her and Percy repair the fence on the old Ryan place on weekends, and maybe even for a while that summer!

Tex raised his hand and rubbed his bristly hair. "I'd have to ask my dad," he said. Then he yawned. He did not seem to care much. Gussie was surprised.

"Don't you even want to?" she asked.

"Don't make a bit of difference to me," Tex said, yawning. "Nothing to do out there, is there?"

"*Nothing* to *do!* Hunt for treasure and look for the lake monster, that's all!"

Tex laughed. "Grant, you're off your gourd!" he said. "You might find a fortune in bedsprings in Ryan's old dump, or a monster coyote, but that's about all. There's your mother's car. See you around."

48

"But will you do it?"

"Okay. Big deal," he said.

Gussie yelled after him, as he marched away, "Bring your toothbrush and stuff to school Friday so you can go home with us!"

Tex walked on without answering.

9

Tex brought a bedroll and an Army pup tent to the Grants', plus a little sack that he called a ditty bag. It had his father's name and Navy serial number stenciled on it, and contained toothbrush, pajamas, and such things. He said he would rather sleep outside and be able to see the stars. Gussie wanted to, too, but the Grants had no camping supplies. She helped Tex pitch his tent on the grass below her window.

On his bedroll, he laid out a mess kit, flashlight, comb, toothbrush and toothpaste, and a combat knife with jagged knuckles on it. He stabbed the knife into the ground by the tent.

Gussie gritted her teeth when she saw it. Was he going to tell her how many frogs he had stabbed with it?

Mrs. Grant served meat loaf, baked potatoes, and pie.

After eating, Tex said: "That was good chow, Mrs. Grant. It's the first meal I've had in two months that wasn't frozen."

"Even breakfast?" Gussie challenged.

"I have a couple of Frosty Pop-Ups for breakfast. Frozen pizza, sometimes."

He helped clear the table, and prepared for bed. After Gussie was ready for bed, she opened the bedroom window and leaned out to yell at him:

"Good night, Tex!"

"Good night, Grant," a voice from the tent said.

Gussie got her French horn and lugged it to the window. Then she yelled down: "Now hear this! I'm going to play Taps."

The notes went rolling across the hills. After she had finished, Tex called up to her:

"That was pretty good. Where did you learn—?"

A far-off cry checked him. Gussie shivered when she heard it. It was the same wild howl she had heard the first night she was here! The sound was like cries she had heard at the zoo.

For a long time there was no sound from Tex. Then he put his head out of the tent and gazed around. Finally he looked up, his face pale in the moonlight. "Did you hear that echo?" he asked.

Gussie swallowed. "Yes."

"It didn't sound much like Taps, did it?"

"No."

"I guess the echoes came from lots of different places, and they got scrambled."

"I guess so," Gussie said. "Well, good night, Tex."

She saw his hand come out of the tent and retrieve the combat knife stuck in the ground by the tent flap. She was glad she was sleeping inside tonight.

Percy and Al came by during breakfast. The Grants and Tex were eating by the window in the big kitchen. Mrs. Grant had begun to make progress in cleaning up the grime of years around the stove and sink. Percy accepted a cup of coffee and sat down.

"Heard yesterday the sheep shearers will be along early next month," he said. "You'd better get busy fixing up your loafing shed, Tom."

"What's a loafing shed?" asked Gussie.

"Where you pen your sheep before shearing. Otherwise, if it rains, or the sheep decide to go wallowing in a creek, they'll be too wet to shear. Even a heavy fog's bad for shearing."

"I haven't taken a good look at it," said Mr. Grant. "What's it need?"

"New roof, for one thing. Metal's best. And it needs some reframing."

"Excuse me while I break into tears," said Mr. Grant. "That's more money you're talking about."

"The store will carry you till you sell some lambs." Percy got up. "Let's get to work, kids! The boss ain't paying you to sit here eating doughnuts."

They drove away in his pickup truck. Gussie took her French horn along, because she thought she might practice at lunchtime. The country road snaked along a ridge for a while, then doubled back toward the ocean. Where it turned left, they swung right onto a little dirt road. A locked gate stopped them after a few yards. As Percy got out to open the gate, he pointed to a small lake below them.

"That's Loony Lake," he said. "There—in that little grove of firs."

Gussie saw the lake, like a blue-green cucumber, at the bottom of the ridge. On the sides of the little valley in which it lay there were light green meadows and patches of dark green fir trees. And there were old orchards gleaming with new leaves.

"Why do they call it 'Loony'?" asked Tex.

"Because loons used to nest there. That's a sort of duck. Don't see many of them nowadays. They have a real crazy cry. Makes you want to check the lock on the door."

The children's glances met and darted away. They were both thinking of the cry last night.

"Are there any loons there now?" asked Gussie.

"Don't believe so."

Then what did we hear? Gussie wondered.

Percy locked the gate behind them and drove down the hill. Gussie gazed at the little valley and the lake below. Although small, the lake was very deep, Percy said, and the water was icy and dark. A brook flowed into the upper end of it, and the lower end was marshy and wet. At the bottom of the hill, the road was very bad. But Percy's truck had four-wheel drive, and he was able to plow easily through the boggy places.

"Good trout fishing in the lake," he said. "But nobody fishes here because of the, er, stories. I haven't been over here since your uncle, er, died."

"What was he doing over here, if he didn't use the place anyway?" Tex asked.

"He was planning to use it for hogs. When the accident happened, he was grading for a loading ramp. Right up yonder—"

He stopped the truck and pointed up the hillside. Gussie could see where the earth was rumpled from some grading. Tall grass had grown over the scars. Nearby there was a large shrub with blue flowers. Although it was some distance from the tractor marks, Gussie saw that it had been badly mauled and half its branches were gone.

"Did you see the monster footprints?" she asked.

Percy did not reply for a while. "Saw something," he muttered. "Big footprints in the dirt. About so gross—" His hands made the shape of a tennis racket.

"Gosh!" Gussie said.

"Bear tracks," Tex shrugged.

"No, no—bigger than bear tracks. Plus, they were webbed—like a duck's feet!"

Webbed! Gussie thought. That meant it was a creature that lived in the water! But a creature with feet a foot and a half long! What could you call a water-dwelling animal like that but a lake monster?

Tex finally spat out the window and said, "Probably somebody on snowshoes."

10

THE ROAD skirted the woods and climbed the hillside. They passed an old apple orchard with gray branches and green leaves. Below, the firs fringed the lake. Percy stopped beside a tumbledown cabin in a clearing on the hillside. Near it were a ragged gray woodpile and an out-side toilet. On the slope, a dozen crooked gray fruit trees huddled together like old soldiers. The old cabin had never been painted, and the wood had bleached to the soft gray of a silver fox.

"This was Ryan's place," Percy said.

"The one that was going to deck his wife in furs and diamonds?" Gussie asked excitedly.

"Him."

"No furs or diamonds here," said Tex. "Diamondback rattlesnakes, maybe. Fur coats on squirrels."

Percy grubbed in the back of the pickup, clattering heavy metal tools like bars of iron against the truck's steel sides. Gussie was ashamed of Tex for being so scornful of Percy's stories. He had had enough faith in lake creatures last night to sleep with a trench knife beside him.

At last Percy produced a strange-looking affair that resembled a skinny vacuum cleaner with a pair of headphones at the end of a cord. "There she is!" he said.

"There what is?" Gussie asked.

"Metal detector. Picks up signals if there's any gold or iron in the ground. Listen to this—"

He threw a pair of wire cutters on the ground and adjusted the headphones to Gussie's ears. All she heard was a faint throbbing sound. Then Percy swept the flat head of the detector, which was like a huge phonograph record, over the tool. Immediately the fluttering sound grew faster, becoming a squeal when the round head was directly over the wire cutters.

Tex wanted to listen, too. He saw a rusty horseshoe lying in the grass and held the detector over it. Gussie took the headphones and listened to the squeal, while Percy unloaded a couple of shovels.

"I won't need you two this morning," he said, "so you can prospect for buried treasure. I've got to dump the posts and hog wire where I'm going to need them, and go back and get a couple more loads. You two scout around. If you get a good signal, dig and see what's making it. Here's your horn." He placed the horn on the woodpile and drove off.

Gussie and Tex took turns prospecting about the cabin, looking as though they were vacuum-cleaning the grass. They got many strong signals in the phones, but all they found when they dug were pieces of rusty iron.

Then they slipped inside the cabin. In one corner, pack rats had raised a gigantic hill of twigs. The wood stove had been smashed to pieces. Earlier treasure hunters had long since torn up the flooring. They decided there was no use looking here, and went out into the sunshine.

"Let's try down by the lake," Gussie suggested. "Ryan probably wouldn't have hidden his treasure so close to the cabin anyway. That's exactly where thieves would look. Let's look along the shore."

Gussie hid her horn inside the cabin. Then they went downhill to the grove, which they had to pass through to reach the lake. Among the trees, big ferns grew up from the soft earth, standing tall and jagged in the throbbing silence. A bird kept making sounds like someone trying to sharpen a saw. Squirrels chattered at them. A chilly dusk replaced the golden daylight. Gussie kept gulping down mouthfuls of cool shade. Then they squirmed through a tangle of elderberry bushes to a narrow beach fringed with brush.

Near the shore, water lilies floated in the shallow water and wild rice grew in tangles. Mallards swam farther out in the lake and the little black ducks called mud hens dived in the shallows. It was a beautiful, quiet place. Gussie looked for the prints of big webfeet in the sand, as Tex began sweeping the detector back and forth. Out on the lake a fish flopped, and gnats hovered over the water like smoke.

Suddenly Tex yelled. "Hey! Listen to this!"

He turned one of the phones so that they could both listen. The squeal sounded high and excited in Gussie's ear. Tex swept the detecting head around. As the signal rose and fell, they could picture the shape of the thing that was giving back the signal.

It was at least as large as a door!

"Ryan's Millions," Tex said, with a grin.

Near the water, it passed under a clump of brush. Or *was* it brush? It reminded Gussie of the pack rat's nest in the cabin—a great heap of twigs and branches. But this heap was as large as a washing machine. It looked like an enormous nest. And there was something else peculiar about it: many of the branches from which it had been woven bore the dried remains of blue flowers. Gussie climbed the side of it—and gasped.

"Tex!" She pointed down into the nest.

Tex clambered up the ragged crater, and together they gazed down on a single, apricot-colored egg as big as a football! Tex leaned over to pick it up, but Gussie seized his arm.

"Don't touch it! The mother will throw it out of the nest if she smells us on the egg."

Tex straightened up. And they both gazed silently at the egg, thinking the same thing.

The mother what? Bird? No bird in the world laid eggs that large. They turned to gaze out over the lake.

58

11

A CRASHING in the brush startled them. Gussie uttered a yelp of fright and ran toward an azalea thicket. Tex started to climb a small tree. Then the brush parted, and the hood of a car poked through. Percy drove the pickup onto the damp, hard sand of the shore. He stopped, opened the door, and Al jumped down and ran to the edge of the lake to lap the still, cold water among the water lilies.

"Percy!" Gussie cried. "Look at this—!"

But before they could lead him to the nest, Al began running back and forth on the sand, sniffing the earth, and finally climbed the nest and peered down into it. Then he sat down and began to howl.

"Now what's got into you, you lovely thing?" Percy said.

"There's an egg in there as big as a football!" Tex yelled.

"Prob'ly is a football," Percy said.

He climbed the crater of branches and leaves and gazed down into the nest. Then he removed his hat and with a wadded handkerchief patted the top of his head. Al was still howling. Percy swung his hat at him and the Kelpie lay down and moaned.

"Probably a gourd," Percy said.

Gussie climbed the nest again and gazed intently at the egg. In shape, it fell somewhere between a football and a basketball. In color, it was a rich orange color with pale blue freckles. "It's an *egg!*" she said.

Percy returned to the sand and stood gazing across the lake. "Either it's an old football," he said, "or it's something somebody's put here to fool people. Yep, that's about the size of it—April Fool joke. They want us to carry it to town and tell everybody we found a monster egg, and then they'll say, 'The joke's on you. It's Styrofoam!'"

"Well, why don't we find out?" Tex asked. "If it breaks, it's an egg. If it bounces, it's not."

Percy shook his head. "But if it's an egg, and we break it, it won't hatch out. But it's no egg, kids."

He turned his back on it and glanced around the shore. He began humming to himself. Gussie was astonished at his attitude! She was positive they had found the egg of a lake monster. Yet he obviously did not even want to talk about it!

"Just look at it!" she said. "It *has* to be an egg."

60

Percy blew his nose in a rumpled handkerchief and frowned at the egg. "Maybe it is, maybe it isn't. If it is, it's not from any duck, I'll tell you that."

As he gazed at the egg, Gussie realized that he was somehow worried about it! She saw him glance out over the lake and rub his ear. Then he suddenly asked:

"Did you find anything with the detector?"

Gussie sullenly pointed to the marks she had made on the ground, outlining the shape of their find. Percy took the metal detector and swept it around. Then he took one of the shovels and drove the blade down into the damp sand. Only a few inches beneath the surface, it struck something. He probed around, working closer and closer to the nest. Then he got down on hands and knees and tried to see under the heap of branches.

Finally, without saying anything, he got a rope from the truck, looped it about the nest, and hitched it to the back of the truck. He started the engine and carefully dragged the nest out of the way.

Where it had stood, the hood of an old automobile thrust up out of the sand! The nest had been built on the rounded shape of the hood. The hood was rusty, but large areas of dark green paint still showed.

Percy began to laugh. Al rubbed against him, whimpering as if worried, and baring his front teeth.

"Quite a treasure you've found!" he said. "If I remember rightly, it's an Essex, about a 1936. It's Dr. Jane Wigmore's, the biologist."

"What's it doing here?" asked Tex.

"Dr. Wigmore came up here on a monster hunt,

sometime in the fifties. She was the science teacher in the high school, and she found some footprints and decided to settle once and for all whether there was a monster in Loony Lake. I think she found a few old bones. She brought her car close to the lake to load them into it, and before she could get out, the car began to sink! The more she spun the wheels, the deeper it sank.

"She was stuck for good, so she hiked over to my place. I drove her home, and meant to come out the next day, but it started to rain. Did it rain! There were reports of surf perch swimming up the highway, bumper to bumper. The lake rose, and I never was able to get in with a tractor until the next summer. And by that time Dr. Wigmore said, 'Forget it.' She'd already had to buy a new car, and the old one was at least fifteen years old."

"That's practically an antique," said Gussie.

"Antique cars are worth a lot of money," Tex said. "Maybe it's worth more now than it was then!"

"Hmm. That's true. I could run my little cat over here and snake it right out." A grin wrinkled Percy's small eyes. "Might have a little fun with Jane. I'll work out the details while we eat."

The details were that Gussie and Tex could mend fence for a couple of hours, while he brought the tractor over. Then they would load the Essex on his truck and haul it in town. Should be able to do it before dark, he said.

Percy had scattered metal fence-posts alongside a rotting wooden fence on the hill. He showed them how to use the fencing tool. It had handles, and a socket into which steel fence-posts fitted. The handles were worked up and down and the post was driven into the earth.

Percy left, and they teamed up on the work, each operating a handle. Percy was back in an hour, hauling the tractor on his flatbed truck. Near the lake, he parked the truck and backed the tractor off it. Then he excavated a sort of ramp down into the sand behind the Essex. He cleared away the soil on both sides, so that the old car was revealed. It was a "touring car," he said, like a sedan without a top. Everything seemed to be intact; even the windshield was still in place. With shovels, they hurled the earth out the open doors.

Percy tied the cable to the rear axle of the Essex. He told Tex to take the steering wheel. The wheels grated and squalled as they turned, but Tex was able to steer the car backwards up the ramp, as Percy pulled it with the winch.

While Percy loaded the Essex, Gussie studied the giant egg, pondering what to do about it. The sunlight fell warmly upon it, and she could imagine the creature inside swelling and beginning to peck at the shell. Who would feed it when it came out, since there was no sign of its mother?

She broke off some ferns in the woods, collected a few water-lily blossoms, and tore them all up. She left them in a neat pile beside the egg.

Of course, she told herself, Percy might be right. The egg was probably plastic, left by pranksters.

But in her heart, she was certain it was a real egg.

12

WHEN THEY reached the outskirts of Agate City, Percy parked on the grassy verge of the road beside a gas station, where there was an outside telephone booth.

"Jane only lives a few blocks from here," he said. "But we'll call her first and tease her a little."

He dropped in his dime, then knelt and tilted the receiver so that they could hear what Dr. Wigmore said. The woman who answered sounded out of breath.

"This is Jane Wigmore, hello!"

"Hello, Dr. Wigmore," said Percy, in a deep and mournful voice. "This is Elmer Birdsong, of Birdsong Motors, your local Essex dealer."

The children giggled.

"What?" Dr. Wigmore said. "I don't think I heard you."

"Elmer Birdsong, of Birdsong Motors. I have the new Essex touring car you ordered. I'm sorry it's taken so long, but—"

"*Essex!?* They haven't made Essexes for years. Who did you say this is?"

The children stifled their laughter. Percy's horsey face remained mournful and businesslike as he replied:

"Elmer Birdsong, ma'am. I know they don't make Essexes any more, but this order is dated March, 1937. It's taken quite a while, and I certainly appreciate your patience, Doctor. But the strike held us up."

"*What* strike?"

"The United Valve-Stem Workers. Normally we'd have made delivery within fifteen years, but as I say—"

"Mr. Birdsong, I don't know who you are, or what you're talking about, but I'm watching a rufous-sided towhee, and you'll just have to excuse me."

"It's quite all right, Doctor. The car has been serviced, so if you'll write a check for eight hundred and seventy-five dollars, I'll drive it right over."

Dr. Wigmore was still protesting when he hung up.

They crossed the highway and drove to a small house near the ocean, sheltered from sea winds by a line of dark green myrtle trees. An old lady wearing slacks and a red windbreaker sat on the porch with a pair of binoculars on a strap around her neck. Gussie saw her train the binoculars on them. Then she came down the steps and approached the Essex.

"Percy, you're a darling!" she cried. "My old Essex! How in the world—?"

Percy said, "These are my associates, Jane—Gussie Grant and Tex Fuller. They found it, and I dragged it out. It came to us that you might like to clean the old rig up and restore it. It's an antique now, you know."

Dr. Wigmore put her hands on her hips and gazed at the old car with affection. The luster of the green panels and fenders had dimmed to a chalky finish, now that the water had dried. "Wasn't it a *classy* little car, Percy? I loved that little Essex. You bet I'll clean it up, and I'll keep it in the barn as a museum piece. Thank you."

She insisted on their coming inside for a bite to eat. As they ate, she said:

"And Gussie, what are you interested in?"

Gussie brushed crumbs off her lap. "I'm learning to play the French horn, and I'm going to join the Girl Scouts, and next fall Tex is going to try to get me on the school baseball team, but—" Gussie took a breath, her heart beating faster, because she was coming to what she was really interested in. "—But what I'm really interested in—"

She glanced at Tex, who was listening critically. "—Is lake monsters!" Tex scoffed.

Dr. Wigmore was just setting her teacup down on the saucer. Her hand jerked and the cup nearly overturned. "Why, what an idea!" she said. "I suppose, like all children, you're interested in peculiar creatures and the like—"

"Yes, ma'am, and in whether there really are any monsters in Loony Lake."

Dr. Wigmore gazed at her sharply. "Don't you think

66

'monster' is really a ghost-story word?" she said. "To an ant, a horned toad is a monster. To a horned toad, a boy collecting lizards is a monster. What does 'monster' mean to you?"

Gussie chewed the tip of one of her braids. "Something bigger than I am, and—"

"Like Tex?" Dr. Wigmore smiled.

Gussie grinned at him. "No, as big as a truck, and mean, and scaly, and—"

"Something that might kill you if it caught you?"

"Like the thing that caught Gussie's uncle," said Tex boldly. "My dad says there *is* something in the lake, and that it tipped the tractor over on him! He says he saw the footprints, and he's going to kill it if he ever sees it. But I don't really believe there's anything there, myself."

Dr. Wigmore sighed. "Oh, my. People always want to kill things bigger than they are. But what if this monster were a gentle beast—like an elephant, or a whale? Wouldn't it be too bad to kill it?"

Percy chuckled. "You're just a do-gooder, Jane. Everybody who owns a rifle says so. You won't let them kill eagles if you can stop them, and you'd probably start a Society to Protect the Loony Lake Monster if you thought anybody would join! But it's a fact, Jane: There *were* footprints there, because I saw them!"

"So did I," Dr. Wigmore said quietly. "I went out by myself and made plaster casts of them, before the rain washed them out. While the monster-haters were out creeping around the lake with rifles, I was making casts and looking for clues to what had happened. What I found was that the prints were made *before* the tractor tipped over on Gussie's uncle! The prints were *underneath* the tractor. So the creature was there before he came along, and had already left. It's not at all unusual for tractors to tip over in hilly country like this. Your uncle just had the misfortune to have it roll over on him."

Gussie's mouth dropped open. She felt pumped up with excitement. So there *was* a monster!

Dr. Wigmore stood up and pulled off her red windbreaker. "I'm going to show you something, now. But first you must promise to join my club, and not tell what you've seen. Anybody who doesn't will have to wait outside. I know Tex's father is a monster-hater, so maybe he won't want to join. I won't hold it against him if he doesn't. But the rules of the club don't allow monster-haters."

Embarrassed, Tex rubbed the bristly top of his head. "What's the club called?" he asked.

"The Friends of the Loony Lake Monster," Dr. Wigmore said. "We are devoted to finding out if there *is* a monster, and to protecting it if there is. We're a sort of Audubon Society, only we protect lake creatures instead of birds. If we can find any to protect."

"How many members do you have?" Percy asked.

"One—me. There'll be four, if all of you join."

Gussie immediately raised her hand. Percy grinned and raised his, and everyone looked at Tex. After a moment, Tex stood up. "I'll wait outside," he said.

"I've seen pictures of monsters, and I don't think they need friends. I don't think there is a monster, but if there is I'm not going to be its friend."

Tex went out, his back straight and stiff. Gussie wrinkled her nose.

Dr. Wigmore said, with a smile, "He's just being loyal to his father. But we're going to be loyal to our monster. Now I'm going to show you something I've never dared show anyone else—"

She led them into a small study lined with books and shelves. Then she closed the curtains and turned on a desk lamp, creating an air of mystery that made Gussie tingle. On the shelves she saw old bones—fossilized fish engraved on bits of stone, skeletons of small animals, and a number of Indian pots. There were also prints of birds, as well as bird nests and eggs and a whole row of books about birds.

Dr. Wigmore opened the door a crack and looked out as though checking for spies. She closed it again and said in a whisper:

"Now I'm going to show you a picture of the Loony Lake Monster!"

Gussie held her breath as the biologist took a large book from a shelf. A purple ribbon marked a page in it. Laying it on the desk, she opened the book to a picture of a heavy-bodied, long-tailed animal, like a lizard standing on heavy hind legs. It had tiny front legs. Its head was similar to a duck's, but with a little dome on the top with two holes in it, apparently for breathing. Just below the breathing holes was a pair of eye sockets.

" 'Camptosaurus,' " Dr. Wigmore read aloud. " 'A medium-sized dinosaur about eight feet high.' See the breathing holes in the top of its head? That's the main clue that my monster descended from Camptosaurus."

"*Your* monster?" Gussie said, puzzled. "Did you really find one?"

"Part of one, at least!"

From a closet, Dr. Wigmore brought a box containing a large fragment of old bone with brown stains. It resembled half of a flattened cantaloupe, with two large holes in the top of it, and, just below them, two eye sockets.

"Look at this piece of bone," she said, "and then compare it with the head of Camptosaurus in the book! They're almost identical. I found this piece of bone in the mud the day I lost my Essex. It's part of an animal that used to live in Loony Lake."

Gussie handled the piece of bone, putting her fingers in the eye sockets and breathing holes. With those holes the animal could breathe while submerged; and with the eyes set so high in its head, it could see above the water, like the captain of a submarine through a periscope.

"But if this was from a Camptosaurus," Gussie said suddenly, "that would mean your monster was a dinosaur, wouldn't it?"

"Yes. And if there is a monster in Loony Lake now, it would be a descendant of the dinosaurs, too. But then, so are turtles and lizards."

Dr. Wigmore returned the piece of bone to the box.

"Land sakes," Percy said. "Dinosaurs in Curry County!"

Dr. Wigmore glanced out the door again and reclosed it. Gussie sensed that she was about to tell them another secret.

"Would you like to see how my monster looked when it was alive?" Dr. Wigmore asked. Gussie clapped her hands together. Dr. Wigmore brought another box from the closet. This one was about the size of a portable record player. She removed its cover to reveal a miniature diorama, with every tiny plant in perfect detail. A lake lapped a sandy shore, and in the shallows an animal like Camptosaurus stood on its hind legs with some uprooted plants in its forepaws.

Dr. Wigmore explained that her monster was a little different from Camptosaurus, the feet webbed, the forelegs smaller. She explained why she had made these changes, but Gussie didn't understand everything she said, and besides, she was thinking of something else.

"Did Camptosaurus and your monster lay eggs?" she asked.

"All dinosaurs laid eggs. We have a number of fossilized dinosaur eggs in museums."

"Dr. Wigmore," Gussie said, dramatically, "I've got news for you. We've got one of your monster's eggs! We found it near your car today!"

13

Dr. Wigmore insisted that Gussie draw a picture of the egg with a set of pastel pencils. Gussie sketched while Percy examined the diorama and Dr. Wigmore flipped through books filled with pictures of bird eggs. She would look at what Gussie was drawing, then compare it with something in a book.

"That's close," she would mutter. "But the ostrich egg is only about five inches in diameter, and you say yours is at least ten. Here's one! You're sure of the color of your egg?"

"It was orange, with blue specks."

At the desk, Gussie worked on, her tongue poking out the corner of her mouth. At last it was finished. She had even drawn a picture of the nest, complete with its blue flowers. Dr. Wigmore studied it under the desk lamp. Outside, the sun was going down, and the only light in the room came from the small, green-shaded lamp.

"Well, dear," said Dr. Wigmore, "I'm afraid practical jokers have been at work. In the first place, I don't think amphibious creatures would build nests. In the second place, the color seems too bright to be natural. It wouldn't be the first time somebody had played practical jokes in this county. Once they even sewed lizard legs onto a dead snake and brought it to me to identify."

"But what about the nest?" Gussie argued.

"What about it, dear?"

"Why would a practical joker go so far to get leaves and branches to build a nest, when there are plenty right there on the beach?"

Dr. Wigmore looked puzzled. "Where do you think he got them, if not on the beach?"

Gussie flapped the picture she had drawn of the nest. "Didn't you see the blue flowers on the nest? There *aren't* any bushes with blue flowers near the lake! But there's a bush with blue flowers near where the tractor tipped over. And it's all broken up, as if something had torn out branches for a nest!"

"That's a fact, Jane," said Percy. "I figured a bear had tore it up."

Dr. Wigmore studied the picture closely. "Good heavens! Most animals *do* have favorite nesting materials. Could the animal have been up there on the hillside, hunting branches for its nest, before the accident happened? And after the accident, when all the hunters had left, perhaps it went back and got the materials for its nest."

"But in that case," said Percy, "where is the critter now?"

"I can't imagine. Unless some hunter shot it later when it was submerged, not realizing what it was. They'll shoot at anything that moves and doesn't wear a red hat around here."

Percy cracked his knuckles. "They shot at four things that *were* wearing red hats last deer season," he said. "Hunters. I don't even go hunting any more, it's got so—"

"Or maybe the monster moved to a new home like we did," Gussie said quickly. "Maybe it didn't like all the excitement around Loony Lake and walked up the creek to the next lake."

"That could be," Dr. Wigmore agreed. "There are lakes all over these hills. Well, dear, I'll come out soon and look at it. But I don't dare spend much time there, because people think of me as the Monster Lady, and if there really *is* an egg, and they see me going back and forth, they'll follow me out there and destroy it."

When they reached the ranch, Gussie's mother came out and insisted that Percy and Tex stay for dinner. "It's nothing fancy," she said, "and I burned the beans. But we'd love to have you."

Percy followed her into the house. The anvil still

stood before the sofa. Mrs. Grant waved her dish towel at it. "Crazy thing. Tom's always too busy to move it, and I wasn't built for lifting anvils."

Percy rubbed his hands together. "I'll take care of it right now! Won't take a minute to put it out on the porch, Fern."

Mr. Grant wanted to help him, but Percy squatted, caught the anvil under its long snout and square heel, and lifted. Gussie could have sworn she heard the flooring groan under him. His face red and straining, he took several plodding strides toward the door.

Then, just as he reached the middle of the room, there was a splintering sound. Percy went off-balance. "Woops!" he muttered. The crackling of wood grew louder, and before their eyes Percy began to sink through the floor! Mrs. Grant put her hands over her eyes and screamed. A hole had opened under the rug, and Percy and the rug were sinking through it!

He had sunk to his hips before he released the anvil, which vanished with a deafening roar of breaking wood. Glass crashed in the basement. Dust rose in gray billows. Percy sank out of sight after the anvil, pulling the rug down with him. Where he had stood, there was now a ragged hole in the floor.

Gussie flopped on the floor and squinted down into the basement. "Percy!" she yelled. "Are—you—all—right?"

More glass shattered on a cement floor. A muted voice came up. "I'm fine! Just remembered something—

75

Fred told me the powder-post beetles had ate away all the subflooring. Would somebody hand me down a flashlight?"

Al lay with his head and forefeet hanging over the edge of the hole, howling mournfully into the blackness. Gussie could smell pickle relish. She turned to yell at her father,

"Get a rope! No—get two ropes and some pieces of wood, and we'll make a rope-ladder for him to climb up on. . . ."

"Relax, supergirl," her father said. "We're going to turn on the cellar light and let him walk up the stairs."

14

THEY ALL agreed, at dinner, that it was not Percy's fault. The fact was, Percy confided, powder-post beetles had undermined the floor of the entire house. He said that Uncle Fred had had an estimate of four thousand dollars for the repairs. The rotted flooring would have supported him or the anvil, but not both.

Gussie saw her father lay down a forkful of burned beans and look at her mother. "Four thousand dollars!" he said.

"Well, it doesn't have to be done right now," Mrs. Grant said cheerfully. "We can put a piece of plywood over the hole, and not bring in things that are too heavy, and—"

"—And maybe all wear water wings filled with helium, so we'll walk lighter," Mr. Grant growled.

Gussie looked at Percy, who was not eating much. The food was really terrible. Tex, who was used to terrible food, was the only one who was eating with any appetite. Gussie decided it might be a good time to mention the giant egg, since no one would be distracted by the food.

"Guess what we found today!" she said. "A monster egg!"

"How big?" laughed her father. "Fifty pounds? I'd like to order a dozen, and we'll put up jars of scrambled eggs for nights when the beans are burned."

Gussie was going to estimate a hundred pounds, but her mother came in wearily: "Guess what *I* found today! A monster tax bill—right in the mailbox. Eleven hundred dollars!"

Gussie's father choked on a bite of biscuit. Then he carried his plate to the sink and stood looking out the window into the night.

"Taxes," he said, "and fencing, and a new loafing shed, and hogs— Fern, is my crying towel back from the laundry?"

Percy picked at a broken fingernail. "Going to need culverts before you can haul in wood for the shed, too," he muttered. "Fred was planning to cut some trees over there, but the logger couldn't go in because the road was washed out."

Gussie saw her father shudder. "This may be the shortest sheep-ranching career in history," he sighed.

Gussie sat frowning at her plate. What they were thinking about, she knew, was going back to the city.

Where nothing ever happened. Where the air was like a dragon's breath. Where her father hated his work.

"I can sell my horn," she said.

Her father shrugged. "There's fifty dollars right there. Now we only owe ten thousand."

Tex dumped some more ketchup on his beans and looked at Percy with a grin. "How about Ryan's Millions?" he said. "If we can find that, the Grants will be rich."

Percy looked embarrassed. "Well, now, I wouldn't count on much money there," he confessed. "I figure there's a little money buried somewhere, but— Well, the fact is, Ryan made his own beer and never owned better than a fifteen-year-old automobile in his life, so he couldn't have been what you call rich."

"Then what about those trees your uncle was going to cut?" Tex asked Mrs. Grant. "Why not cut them and pay your bills? My dad says a Douglas fir is money in the bank."

Silence flowed in; everyone looked shocked. Gussie heard coals snapping in the stove. Percy looked up in surprise, and Mr. Grant turned from the window with a smile dawning on his face.

"Percy," he said, "somebody just said something intelligent. *Are* there trees to cut? I thought it was mostly pasture."

Percy looked stunned. "Funny I never thought of that! Sure, there are trees—tucked into the ravine along Bullet Creek, between your ranch and Andrews Timber Company's tree farm."

Mr. Grant whooped. "Let the helium out of your water wings, folks!" he yelled. "We'll pay the taxes, buy the hogs, and maybe even get a gas stove that doesn't burn the beans!"

Percy said there was plenty of equipment around the place to do the logging themselves and not have to divide the tree money with some logging company. They would start tomorrow, while Gussie and Tex drove fence-posts.

15

IN THE MORNING, Mr. Grant drove Gussie and Tex to the hillside where they had been working. Percy had telephoned to say that he would be over later. Gussie wanted to show her father the egg, but he said he had too many things to do to waste time on an Easter egg hunt. He would come back for them about three o'clock, he said, unless Percy had time to come over. He drove away.

They set posts until noontime.

Mrs. Grant had made sack lunches for them, and they sat down to eat near the cabin. Tex lay back on the warm green grass. A bird in the grove was making loud whacking calls, like someone chopping wood.

"Nice out here," he said.

Gussie looked at him in surprise. Was he beginning to soften up a little?

"It's nice of you to help us build the fence, Tex. I don't know how much Daddy can pay you, but it will be better than nothing."

"If you were worried about me telling people you found the egg, I won't. Anyway, I think it's just plastic."

Gussie smiled to herself. "Do you mind if I practice my French horn?"

"No. Can you play anything besides Taps?"

Gussie got up. The horn came gleaming from its case. It was much too large for her, but she would grow, and the horn would not, so eventually they would be a perfect match. She braced herself against the old rail fence, took a breath, and blew. The notes floated out clear and strong. She played the beginning of the *Surprise Symphony*. As Tex pretended to applaud, she pretended to take a bow.

And then they heard the call from the lake.

It was high and honking, more of a squawk than a call. It was much higher than the sounds they had heard the other night. It sounded three times, then stopped. Tex scrambled to his feet, staring down the hill. Gussie raised the horn to her lips and sounded a few more notes.

The call came again.

She dropped the horn and began to run down the hill. "It's hatched!" she yelled. When she looked back, Tex was following, his face grim, the fencing tool in his hands like a club.

82

Gussie streaked through the woods to the lakeshore. For a moment she hid in a clump of ferns to make sure no giant lizard with blazing eyes was rising from the lake. But her eye was immediately caught by a movement in the nest.

Above its rim rose a gray-green head with a bill like a duck's. It swerved about, its bill opening and closing. *It's alive! It's alive!* Gussie thought. *And it's mine!* She stepped into view.

"Here I am!" she called.

The greenish head swiveled toward her. Immediately, the little animal started moving about in excitement. The beak opened and closed, uttering little trumpetings.

Gussie ran to the nest and looked down inside it. "Hello!" she said.

The creature looked exactly like the model of Dr. Wigmore's! It was somewhat like a kangaroo, with a long thick tail, strong hind legs, and a long neck. Its head was like a duck's, but larger, with a little dome atop it. It had big duck-feet. And the strange thing was that it acted as though it had been waiting for Gussie to appear, for it kept thrusting its open beak toward her, like a baby bird asking for food.

And suddenly she understood. That was exactly what it *was* doing! The little pile of green leaves and blossoms she had left in the nest was gone. Nothing remained but fragments of apricot-colored eggshell.

As she hastily gathered water-lily blossoms along the shore, Tex came running up. "Where is it?"

83

"Can't you see it?" Gussie panted. "It's in the nest!"

"No, it isn't."

Gussie looked around. The creature had vanished! She ran back and found it crouching on the bottom of the nest, its eyes closed. She reached down and touched its head, which was cold and smooth.

"It's all right, baby. Here's something to eat."

Hearing her voice, the animal rose cautiously and accepted a beakful of greens. But when Tex came near, it sank down again and pretended to go to sleep. Tex peered down at it.

"Son of a gun!" he whispered.

Gussie beamed. She had just realized something wonderful. The baby thought she was its mother! It trusted her, but not Tex. She told Tex:

"Back off. I want to make an experiment."

As Tex did so, she leaned over the animal and said, "It's all right now."

Hearing her voice, the creature rose, took some water lilies from her hand, and chomped contentedly on them.

"See that?" Gussie said. "It thinks I'm its mother!"

Tex scratched his neck, looking doubtful. "What do you mean?"

"What's the first thing a baby bird sees when it comes out of the shell?" Gussie said. "Its mother. We read in science class in Los Angeles where a man raised birds from eggs, and when they saw him they thought he was their mother, because he was the first thing they saw. It's called, 'imprinting.' As long as she lives, Jane will think I'm her mother!"

84

"Jane?" said Tex. "Why do you call her that?"

Gussie gazed fondly at the hungry little lake monster, the only one of its kind, probably, in the entire world. "It's a *Camptosaurus wigmorii*," she explained. "And Dr. Wigmore's name is Jane, so that's what I'm naming her."

Fifteen minutes later, Jane was fast asleep. Gussie picked out the shell fragments to save for Dr. Wigmore. Thoughts were tumbling about her mind like laundry in a clothes drier. So many things to decide!

"How often do you suppose it eats?" she asked Tex, as they sat near the nest.

"All the time, probably, like baby birds. That's your main problem, Grant. How will you get out here to feed it?"

"Well, school will be out in two weeks. Probably Percy will feed her for me until then. Listen," Gussie said, looking closely at Tex, "are you going to tell everybody?"

He shook his head. "Scout's honor. I'll even join the Friends of the Loony Lake Monster. Because there are a lot of creeps in this country who'd come up here and hack it to pieces, just for souvenirs!"

"Then the only problem will be feeding her." Gussie's mind was clicking along like an electric train. "There's that old saddle horse I used to ride when we'd visit Uncle Fred—Frisky. Can't I ride him back and forth?"

Tex grinned. "Frisky? Sure. Only trouble with him

is he's frisky like a tortoise. You'll have to take along a bucket of coffee when you go riding to keep him awake."

"Okay, I'll come over here after school every afternoon and feed Jane, and Percy can do it in the morning." Gussie got up and looked down at Jane sleeping. "Isn't she cute?" she said.

Tex regarded the animal with amusement. "Yes, but take my advice, Grant—don't get too attached to her. In about a week she'll dive into the lake and you'll never see her again. Face it, kid—she's just a lizard, and she'll forget all about you."

Gussie smiled dreamily. "She'll *never* forget me, Tex, because I was the first thing she ever saw!"

"Dream on. The first thing I ever saw was my old man opening a can of beer. But that doesn't mean I run up to him and ask for a swig of beer every time I see him!"

16

Jane woke again and asked to be fed, wobbling about the nest with her beak gaping as she made her urgent bugling sounds. Once, Tex offered her some water-lily leaves, but she hid in the bottom of the nest and pretended to sleep until Gussie spoke to her. Even then, she would not accept food from Tex's hand, but waited until he dropped it into the nest and backed off.

Gussie felt very warm and protective. She was the only person in the world Jane trusted! Then she remembered that mother birds had distress calls, and feeding calls, to let their nestlings know how to behave in certain situations.

A brilliant idea dawned.

She got her horn from the cabin, and sent Tex to hide behind a tree. Jane plodded clumsily around the nest on her big webbed feet, her head wobbling on its long neck.

"Okay!" Gussie called.

As Tex came into view from behind the tree, Gussie blew the first notes of Taps. The sound startled Jane just at the instant when she saw Tex. She sank down.

After a moment Gussie blew the first notes of the *Surprise Symphony* and then leaned over the nest. "It's all right, now," she said.

Jane roused and blundered clumsily onto her hind legs, and Gussie gave her some water lilies.

They played the horn game for a half hour.

Then Gussie made a test. She told Tex to hide. Jane moved about the nest. She was getting stronger and actually growing larger, as her body, long compressed in the egg, expanded. Gussie blew the first three notes of Taps. Instantly, Jane sank down and closed her eyes! Like a nestling, she had learned to connect the distress call with danger, even when there was no danger.

A moment later, they heard the distress call of an automobile: a horn was honking up on the hillside where they had been working. Someone had come back for them.

It was Percy. When they came gasping up the hill, he was checking one of the new fence-posts. Nearby, Al chewed on a leg bone of some long-dead animal.

Gussie screeched: "Percy! It's hatched! It's hatched!"

Percy gazed at them, his face sad. "I was afraid of that," he said.

88

"Why?"

"Because I've lived so long in a world without monsters that it'll be a while before I can believe in them."

"You'll believe in *her*, Percy! Come on!"

On the lakeshore, Gussie tied Al to a tree to keep him from attacking the baby monster. Al sat there and howled.

Percy waited while Gussie blew the all-clear notes on her French horn. Jane's head appeared. Gussie blew the distress call, and Jane vanished.

"Now you can look at her," Gussie said proudly.

Percy gazed down at the naked, clumsy-looking beast in the nest. Gussie heard him mutter, "Just shows to go you." He took out his handkerchief and blew his nose. Then he turned away.

"Yep," he said. "Just like I thought. It's going to take a while for me to get used to the idea. I'll let you know when I decide to believe in that thing, Gussie."

"Well, will you feed her for me every morning, while you get around to believing in her? She likes ferns, and those shiny leaves over there, and water lilies. If you just drop them in the nest, she'll eat them after you leave. She probably won't eat while you're here, because she'll be afraid of you."

"Oh, she's got to get used to me, too, eh? Well, that makes us even. I don't believe in her, and she don't believe in me."

Riding home, Gussie said suddenly: "Percy?"

"That's me."

"Will you help me find that horse of Uncle Fred's before dark? And show me how to saddle it? That way, I could ride over every day after school and feed Jane, while you're helping Daddy."

Mr. Grant was still working on the loafing shed, so Gussie's mother took Tex home. From the barn Percy got a bridle, and they walked downhill past the apple orchard. It ended at a little creek. A few sheep grazed in the orchard.

"There he is," Percy said.

Near a large stump, an old white horse stood motionless, watching them come. He switched his tail once, and ducked his head. Percy walked up to him. He thrust his thumb between the horse's jaws, and Frisky opened his mouth. Percy eased the bit in place. After that he looped the bridle over Frisky's head. He told Gussie to stand on the stump so that she would be tall enough to mount.

"You'll have to find a stump or a fence when you want to mount. You'd better ride bareback, because you're too little to saddle him."

Gussie rode up the hill, thrilled, aware of Frisky's body moving under her, of his warm hide. The ground was so far below! She felt tall and strong and only a little bit afraid.

17

Suddenly Fern Hill Ranch was as busy as a beehive. Along Bullet Creek, trees were falling and Percy's chain saw shrieked and droned as he cut them into logs. On Wednesday, he and Mr. Grant took three loads of logs to a sawmill at Agate City. Then they came back and felled some more. A single tree could be worth hundreds of dollars, Percy said.

At the ranch house, a carpenter started work on the new floor. Mrs. Grant ordered an electric stove. And every day, Gussie rode Frisky to Loony Lake and fed and trained Jane. The animal grew a foot a day. She reminded Gussie of one of those crinkled kernels of paper that you put in a saucer of water and watch as it opens into a Japanese flower.

Jane ate pounds and pounds of greens, blissfully chewing each tender leaf and fern frond. Gussie horn-trained her before meals, because afterward she always burped a few times and fell asleep. By Wednesday, Jane was so large she could scarcely turn around in the nest! She looked as cramped as a ten-year-old child in a baby buggy.

But Thursday, at school, Tex had disturbing news.

"This morning my dad asked me who 'Jane' was!" he whispered.

Gussie gasped. "Where did he hear about Jane?"

"I talk in my sleep sometimes," Tex said. "I told him Jane was a girl at school, and he said, 'Attaboy, Tiger!' So he doesn't suspect yet."

The word "yet" troubled Gussie.

Because, eventually, people would have to know. And then what would happen? The first thing would be that some of them would want to shoot Jane, as some people shot eagles—just for fun.

She suddenly remembered Dr. Wigmore.

She telephoned her that afternoon while her mother was chopping kindling for the cookstove and making a terrible job of it. "Dr. Wigmore?" she said in a whisper.

"Yes? I can't hear you very well," said Dr. Wigmore.

Gussie raised her voice a bit. "It's hatched!" she hissed. "It looks like your model. Maybe you'd better come out tomorrow. Good-bye."

Dr. Wigmore was there when Gussie, Tex, and Mrs. Grant drove in the next afternoon, Friday. Mrs. Grant prepared a snack, and Dr. Wigmore talked about birds.

"There are hundreds of varieties in this country," she said. "I thought I might take the children for a bird-walk and point out some of them. We might even find an arrowhead."

"How nice," said Mrs. Grant. "Maybe you'll find a lake monster to show them, too!" And she laughed.

Gussie looked at her closely. But she was only joking.

Dr. Wigmore drove up Old 101 to the turnoff, where Gussie unlocked the gate and they went through. They drove as far as they could on the rough road, but when it got too marshy Dr. Wigmore parked. They started walking through the grove. Dr. Wigmore carried a camera.

"Are you going to tell me what hatched out," she asked, "or surprise me?"

"Surprise you," said Gussie.

"Have you ever seen an alligator, Gussie?"

"Sure, at the zoo."

"Well, alligators hatch from eggs too. Does this—this creature resemble an alligator?"

"Wait and see," said Gussie.

They stopped at the cabin and Gussie got her horn. "What's that for, dear?" Dr. Wigmore asked.

"She's trained to hide when I blow Taps."

"Oh, now, really!" said Dr. Wigmore. "I know you've got a pretty healthy imagination, but—"

They reached the lakeshore.

"Now, I'll blow the distress call," Gussie said, "and she'll hide in the nest. So you'll be able to see her before she starts moving around."

Dr. Wigmore gazed nervously at the nest on the sand. "I guess you know that dinosaurs died out a hundred million years ago," she said. "Yet, to all intents and purposes, a lake monster would be a dinosaur. My problem is that I know a little bit about dinosaurs, and a lot about children's imaginations—"

Gussie smiled politely. Then she blew Taps on the horn. "Well, let's go see how much my imagination has grown since yesterday," she said.

Dr. Wigmore seemed to gather herself. Then she went to the nest and leaned over it. A moment later she spun about, her eyes sparkling with anger.

"That's a very cruel joke to play!" she cried. "There's no egg, and there's no monster! I'm surprised at you, Gussie Grant!"

Gussie ran up and looked into the nest. It was empty! She gazed up and down the shore. "But, it *wasn't* a joke! She's left the nest, that's all!"

Dr. Wigmore looked disappointed and doubtful.

"Hey!" Tex blurted. "Blow the all-clear signal! Maybe she's hiding."

Gussie blew and blew, the notes echoing around the little lake from the hills. There was a sudden threshing of water in the lake, as though a large fish were flopping on the surface. Then, over the water, there came Jane's excited trumpeting. They turned, startled, and saw her coming from far out on the lake. Only her head was visible. When she reached the shallow water, she stopped to nibble a few water lilies. Then she wallowed on, to emerge from the lake with festoons of wild rice and water lilies trailing from her neck.

When she saw Tex and Dr. Wigmore, she started to return to the lake, but Gussie blew the all-clear signal again, and she came on, cautiously.

Dr. Wigmore took pictures of Jane and had Gussie measure her with a tape. She wanted to see her teeth, and Jane let Gussie pry her bill open and exhibit them. They were small, flat, and sharp-edged, like chisels. Jane was unsteady on her hind legs. Frequently she had to sit back on her long, thick tail, like a kangaroo. Whenever Tex or Dr. Wigmore came to within ten or fifteen feet of her, she would begin to edge toward the lake. Then Gussie would have to settle her down.

"Just amazing!" said Dr. Wigmore.

"But what if somebody sees her?" asked Gussie, offering Jane a water lily.

Dr. Wigmore knelt to get a picture of Gussie and Jane. "One of two things would happen," she replied. "Number One, some idiot would shoot her." She clicked the shutter and advanced the film. "Number Two, some other idiot would kidnap her and sell her to an aquatic show. Either way, it would kill her." She shot another picture. "She belongs here, where her ancestors have always lived. She'd probably die without exactly the right diet, water temperature, and other things her kind are used to."

"What are we going to do, then?" Gussie insisted.

"I'll write some letters to scientists I know and— No, I'd better not. Not yet. My reputation as an eccentric is bad enough as it is. They'd lock me up."

She glanced at her wristwatch. "It's time I got you back home."

But when they tried to leave, Jane came waddling along the shore behind them!

"Good heavens!" said Dr. Wigmore. "*Now* what are we going to do? We can't tie her up, like a dog—"

"Maybe if I blow the horn," Gussie said, "she'll get back in the nest."

She raised the horn to her lips and blew.

Instantly, Jane turned toward the lake, wallowed through the water lilies and trailing plants, and swam out into the deeper water. A moment later nothing could be seen of her but what looked like a piece of bark floating on the water.

They hurried through the woods and back to the car.

As they were swinging from the side road into the main road, a faded red pickup truck came around a turn. Tex gave a yelp of dismay.

"That's Dad's car!" he said. "Wow! I wonder if he decided to check on me—"

Dick Fuller parked in the road and got out. Gussie saw him take a rifle from a rack across his rear window. With his red baseball cap cocked over one eye, he sauntered toward the other car and leaned against the door. Gussie's heart was thumping. What if Jane picked this particular time to start calling her? Could she be heard up here?

"Well, well!" said Dick Fuller, grinning. "What's the Gray-Crested Do-Gooder been doing at Loony Lake? Bringing a load of worms to robins on welfare? Cracking acorns for tired blue jays?"

Dr. Wigmore spoke right back in the same sarcastic tone. "Get away from me with that ugly rifle, Dick Fuller. What are *you* up to? Hunting fawns, with one eye out for game wardens? Setting out poison for baby tree squirrels?"

"I had a report of a bear killing lambs over on Dart Creek. Would you like a bearskin rug for your office?"

"No," said Dr. Wigmore, "but if I ever get a Government Hunter's hide, I'll bet I tan it good."

She put the car back in gear, and Fuller stepped back, laughing. "And I'll bet you would too! Tex, I'll see you Sunday night. Behave yourself."

18

THAT WEEKEND Gussie and Tex rammed the last of the fence-posts into the earth, and Mr. Grant and Percy finished cutting trees. Percy said the timber would pay all the current bills and a couple of loans, and even put hogs on the Ryan place. He said he would get the hog wire up now, so Mr. Grant ordered two hundred hogs, to be delivered the next Saturday.

Everyone was happy but Gussie. Her emotions dipped and swerved like barn swallows. In the mornings, she had dreams of being the owner and trainer of the world's only lake monster. Scientists would come to study Jane, and Gussie would have a little grandstand erected, where the audience would sit while she showed Jane off and gave a talk about her habits. She would play the French horn and Jane would frolic before the bleachers, or play in the lake. Maybe, for a dollar, people would be allowed to feed Jane a fern frond. Fronds would be sold at a dollar apiece, also.

But in the afternoons, at the lake, Gussie knew they were in trouble.

To see Jane rip through clumps of greenery was frightening. She ate her weight in ferns and water plants daily. Her body swelled with new flesh. She swam like an otter, spending most of her time in the lake, eating underwater like the little black ducks called mud hens, or browsing along the lakeshore, ready to hide in case of danger.

But it was ridiculous to think that she could be hidden forever. And anyone who saw her, and did not know of her gentle nature, would go away raving that he had almost been killed by a man-eating lake monster.

Jane's parents had probably survived, Dr. Wigmore said, because they had lived here for a hundred years, maybe more, and had learned, as settlers came in, to stay out of sight. But Jane had been born into a world already crowded.

Was there room left for a dinosaur?

One night there was a telephone call for Mr. Grant.

It was from Mr. Flugler, the director of the advertising agency where he had worked. Mr. Grant motioned to his wife and daughter to listen while they talked.

"How are things up there in soggy old Oregon?" asked Mr. Flugler.

"Just fine, Luther," Mr. Grant said. "A little wet,

maybe, but that's only during certain months of the year."

"Ah, yes," said Mr. Flugler. "I've heard about your climate. Eleven months of winter, and one month that you couldn't call summer. Are you as happy grazing among the sheep as you expected to be?"

"Well, there *have* been problems," Mr. Grant admitted.

"I'm sorry to hear that, Tommie," said Mr. Flugler. "Down here, things have never been better. What sort of problems have you had?"

"You might call them, well, financial. It turns out that sheep are difficult to get rich on."

"Are they, indeed?"

"And the living room floor dropped out from under us—"

"Tut-tut," said Mr. Flugler.

"But we survive from day to day, with God's help," Mr. Grant sighed.

"In that connection," said his old boss, "I wanted to say that we bear you no ill will for leaving us in the middle of the Zephyr Panty Hose campaign. Your slogan, 'Stockings are clumsy, It's panty hose for Mumsy,' has been turned down by the client. But it was a good try. In any event, Tom-Tom, your old job is waiting for you when you get tired of playing rancher. You weren't exactly a ball of fire, but you were reliable. You did your work—like the cleaning women, ha-ha."

"You're nice to say it, Luther," said Mr. Grant. His face, Gussie observed, was growing red.

"And if you can be back at the desk by a week from Monday, we'll put you on the payroll again. So what do you say, Tombo?"

"What I say," Mr. Grant said, "is this. Why don't you get yourself a little box about an inch square, you know? And put your lousy job in it. Then stuff it in your left ear. Do you get the picture? And some day when you've got time, drive up to Agate City and visit my new herd of swine. You might find they're your kind of people."

Mrs. Grant sighed as he hung up. "Well, there's one job you don't have to worry about again!" she said.

"That's the whole idea," said Mr. Grant.

Fifteen minutes later, the telephone rang once more.

"This is George Andrews," the caller said. "Of Andrews Timber Company."

Gussie, for some reason, knew immediately that it was going to be bad news. Her father, for one thing, looked alarmed.

"Oh, yes," he said. "You own the tree farm next to me, right?"

"Right and wrong," said George Andrews. "I also own some land on *your* side of Bullet Creek—where you've been cutting trees. I'm sure you didn't know that, Mr. Grant. Most people take the creek to be the property line."

Mr. Grant sagged in the chair. "Why, yes, I thought —I mean, it seemed logical—"

"In other words, you've been cutting my trees, not yours! Of course, I don't intend to sue you, Mr. Grant, as long as you send the timber check to me as soon as it comes. Otherwise, as you may know, I'm entitled to claim double damages for this, er, accident. Good night, Mr. Grant."

Gussie's father sagged into the chair. Gussie, who had been crouching on the floor with her ear near the receiver, lay down and looked at the ceiling in shock.

"Good night, Mr. Andrews," her father said. "Good night, everybody in Agate City. It's been nice knowing you. . . ."

"Oh, Tom!" wailed Mrs. Grant. "What will we do? No—I know—call Percy! Maybe he—"

"—Maybe he's got another big idea? I have no doubt in the world, Fern, that Percy could sit here all night and spin big ideas for us. In short, Percy is what Dick Fuller called him. A dum-dum."

Gussie sat up. "He is not! He's lived here all his life, and I'll just bet Mr. Andrews is wrong, not Percy. I'm going to call him up."

She had expected them to stop her, but both of them seemed to be in some sort of daze. She called Percy. For a moment they had trouble understanding each other, because, it turned out, Percy had dropped the receiver and was talking into the wrong end of it. After Percy had the picture, he said,

"Well, ain't that peculiar! Now, I just know George

is wrong. Your fence is down there by the creek, so how *could* he own the land on your side of it? Tell you what, Gussie: You tell your father I'm going to call a lawyer friend in Portland tomorrow, and get this all straightened out. No sweat, as they say in the city."

"See there?" Gussie said, hanging up. "He says Mr. Andrews is wrong!"

"One of us is wrong," her father said. "And if it's me, supergirl, I'll be calling Mr. Flugler in a couple of weeks to see about getting that little box out of his left ear—"

19

IT WAS too late to cancel the order for the hogs. Mr. Grant and Percy labored the rest of the week patching the fence. Hogs, said Percy, would smell out the smallest hole in the wire and walk right through it.

Early Saturday morning, the day the hogs were due, Gussie and Tex rode over to make sure Jane was out of sight. They took care of her, then waited for the hog trucks at the loading ramp—the grassy mound of earth on the hillside where Uncle Fred had died in the tractor accident.

Soon Percy and Mr. Grant arrived, leading a line of grimy green trucks. The drivers backed the trucks up to the ramp and the gates were opened. Out the hogs went, rooting and snorting. In a very short time, nearly all of them were out of sight in the tan-oak thickets. The trucks drove away.

"Those hogs will be eating acorns till you hear them belching in Josephine County!" Percy said. "You're going to make money on them animals, I guaran-darn-tee you."

Just then Tex pointed up the hill, beyond an old orchard. "Look—there are some hogs up there too! Whose are those?"

Percy squinted, took off his hat, reset it, and glanced at the air to his left. "They're ours, I reckon. What's happened, Tom, is that we missed a hole in the fence somewhere, and they're kind of, you know, scattering. Hmm."

"I see," Mr. Grant said, numbly. "Will they stop at the Mexican border? Because they don't have passports."

"It don't matter. They're on my land, and we can round them up later, when we've checked the fence out again. Won't take more'n a week or two. . . ."

Gussie looked at her father and realized he didn't even care. He was smiling dreamily. He picked up a stick and idly tossed it at a lone hog snuffling for acorns under a tree.

"Sure, Percy, sure," he sighed. "Well, it just shows to go you. Let's go over and finish that loafing shed. In case I'm still in Oregon when the shearers arrive."

"About that timber deal," Percy said, as they headed for the pickup. "My lawyer says there's an angle he's going to check into. Don't worry about a thing."

"No, no," Mr. Grant said. "I'm past worrying. What I'm trying to do, now, is to think of a new slogan for Zephyr Panty Hose. They turned my old one down. What about, 'Light as a feather, In all kinds of weather'?"

20

Gussie knew that things were totally out of hand on Fern Hill Ranch. Like Dr. Wigmore's old Essex, buried in the mud of Loony Lake, the ranch was settling into a swamp of troubles. Anywhere but here, Gussie would have thought that there was nothing else to go wrong. But at Fern Hill, it was only a question of time until something else happened. One more disaster, she knew, and her father would rent a moving van, and they would start packing again. . . .

Every night during the last week of school, she dreamt that they were back in the city. A real estate agent led them to an apartment like a doll's house, and said, "It's a little snug, folks, but it's the only one left in the city."

She did not think she could fit into an apartment

again. Any more than Jane could be squeezed back into that orange-colored shell.

On the day school ended, Tex came out to stay for as long as Gussie's father needed help on the fence. He and Gussie followed the fence, through oak thickets and tangles of brush, all the way up to the highway. But it was like locking the barn door after the horse was stolen, because the hogs had not only scattered all over Percy's ranch, but onto other people's land too! The fences around there were built to keep sheep from straying, not hogs.

Still, in case they ever did round the hogs up again, they would need a pasture for them. So the fencing went on.

A week after school closed, Gussie and Tex were searching for gaps in the hog wire near the Loony Lake gate. The fence here ran beside the road. A concrete pipe brought water from a spring across the highway to the fence side. Where it emptied, a large mudhole had been created. Tender plants grew around it and the mud was shiny and deep.

Now and then, as they worked, Gussie would blow a few notes on her horn to let Jane know everything was all right. She shuddered when she thought of how large the little Camptosaurus was getting. Jane was now taller than she, and so heavy she left prints six inches deep in the mud along the lakeshore! And since she could not spend all day underwater, it was only a

question of time until someone saw her. And then what would happen?

Friday noon, as they were thinking of stopping work to eat their sandwiches, Gussie found out what would happen.

A sound of happy honking suddenly floated up the slope to them! She whirled and gazed down the grassy hill. There, snorting and frolicking, with a lavender water lily and some wild rice draped around her neck, came Jane!

Gussie screamed at her: "Go back! Go back!"

"Holy cow!" gasped Tex. "Blow the horn, quick! There's a car coming."

But the horn lay in the grass a hundred feet down the hill. Gussie raced toward it, as Jane came to meet her. She picked up the horn, but Jane had smelled the mudhole beside the road, and she went right on past her to wade in it with little honks of delight. She sank blissfully into the mud and tore out clumps of tender grass.

Gussie ran up and tugged at her neck. "Go back! Bad girl!" she scolded.

The thrum of a car engine grew closer. Tex tried to push Jane from the rear, but it was like moving a boulder. "Blow the horn!" he panted, continuing to push.

Gussie blew Taps. Immediately, Jane closed her eyes and lay down in the mud, pretending to go to sleep.

"Wow, that's a help!" Gussie said.

"Blow the other call! Wake her up. Then maybe you can lead her back—"

When Gussie blew the all-clear tune, Jane rose, dripping mud, and began clumsily frisking around like an enormous web-footed puppy. Closer still, the car could be heard humming toward them on the road. Gussie ran down the hill a few yards and looked back. Good! Jane had begun to follow. Gussie ran faster. The faster she ran, the faster Jane followed, and at last, as a blue pickup truck appeared, they reached the woods.

Gussie led her all the way to the lake, where she blew the distress signal. Jane obediently waded into the water and disappeared.

Gussie ran back through the woods. They had left Frisky grazing on the hillside. As she climbed onto his back from a stump, she could see two men in red hunters' caps talking to Tex. She kicked Frisky with her heels, and he plodded up the hillside. When she arrived, Tex was sitting on the ground, sullenly eating a sandwich. The men stared angrily across the fence at him. Then one of them looked at Gussie.

"Maybe *you* speak English," one of them said. "Your friend here ain't much help. Look at those tracks!"

As Gussie looked down, Frisky tugged at the reins, and she let him lower his head and crop grass. "I don't see anything," she said.

The man, who was short but had a stomach like Mr. Fuller's, slipped under the barbed wire fence. "Right here—where I've got my finger! See that?"

He had his finger on one of the huge tracks left in the mud by Jane.

"Oh, that," Gussie said. "I think my horse did that."

"Oh, has your horse got duck-feet?" asked the man. "Listen, little girl, I was over here after Fred Hill was trampled to death! And that's the same kind of tracks we found then!"

The other man was tall, with big blond eyebrows that turned up at the corners like mustaches. He said flatly, "Any duck with feet that big could carry more passengers than a jet plane, sister."

Gussie laughed and tried a little charm. "That's funny," she said, smiling at the man.

But he looked just as cold and mean as ever, and now he stared down the slope toward the lake. "It's a well-known fact," he said suspiciously, "that dangerous critters have lived in that lake for years. Man-eating monsters!"

"They didn't eat my uncle, did they?" Gussie said, politely.

Both men looked at her closely. "Oh, you're the Grant girl," the short man said. "Is your father at home?"

Gussie closed one eye in thought. "I think he went to Portland on business," she said.

"Heard about that 'business,'" said the man. "Cut a lot of Andrews' trees, Earl! Can you beat that?"

"Why did you want my father?" Gussie asked.

"Because I want the key to the gate. We're going

down there and make a search. But we aren't going in afoot, and be charged by some mad creature. The least we'll need is a car to take shelter in."

Tex got up. "What you want," he said, "is my father. He's the Government Hunter. But it might be out of season for the kind of thing you think is down there. If it's a duck, you can't shoot it before next fall."

The man with the yellow eyebrows said, "If it's a duck, son, I hope I never see an elephant. Come on, Otey. Let's go get Dick Fuller!"

As soon as the hunters' car left, Gussie began to cry. "They're going to kill Jane!" she wailed.

"Cut it out, Grant," Tex said, but he too looked nervous and unhappy. "We'd better get over to the ranch and tell your dad. It'll be an hour before those men can get back from Agate City. But if I know my old man, he'll be coming up here with his thirty-thirty and a whole box of shells."

Gussie sat there on Frisky, still sniffling. Nothing had gone right for days! "Daddy isn't at the ranch," she said. "He's working on the loafing shed, and it would take almost an hour to get there on Frisky. And my mother was going in town this afternoon to shop."

Tex climbed onto Frisky's back behind Gussie. "Well, the house is on the way to the shed, so we'll go by and see if he came back for nails or—or something. If Percy's helping him, he's sure to run out of *something*."

21

No CARS were at the ranch, however, and Gussie ran into the house, hoping someone, anyone, was there to help her. But no one was. The carpenter had apparently quit for the day. In the living room, big pieces of plywood covered the new floor joists. There was a smell of fresh lumber.

"Well, we'll have to ride over to the shed and hope we can get back to the gate before my old man does," Tex said. "He won't go in afoot either, probably, so he'll have to break the chain that keeps the gate closed. But if he brings a bolt cutter, that won't take long."

They went out and led Frisky to the porch, from which they were able to mount again. But just as they turned the old horse up the road, a pickup truck rushed from the firs down the drive, and Gussie squealed with relief.

"It's Percy!"

Percy parked in the middle of the road and thrust his head out the window. "Where's your dad?" he yelled. "Got some good news for him!"

But Gussie began telling him her news before Percy could get started. "Oh, my," Percy said, when she ran out of breath. "That's bad news. Well, get in, and we'll go find him. If he ain't here, he must be at the shed—"

In the truck, driving down Old 101 toward the sheep pasture, he said:

"Might've been better if you'd told him in the beginning."

"Yes, but I was afraid *he* might want Jane destroyed too!"

Percy shook his head in bafflement. "What are you going to do with a creature like that, Gussie? I mean, she's harmless, unless she accidentally steps on you, now that she's gotten to roaming—"

"Well, we'll have to put up a big fence around the place and—"

"And who's going to pay for that? Big fences cost even more than little fences. You hatched yourself a big problem when that creature climbed out of the egg."

They took a dirt road down a bumpy hillside, near the bottom of which was a long shed with a new metal roof that glared in the afternoon light. New and old wood made its sides a patchwork. At the bottom of the slope a little creek ran between brushy banks, and off to the left Gussie could see where her father and Percy had cut the strip of trees. She could understand how Percy had made the mistake about who owned them, because they were inside Uncle Fred's fence, which followed along the bank of the creek.

When they arrived, Mr. Grant was on the roof of the shed, pounding nails through a sheet of new roofing. Gussie ran through the gate and stood below him. Without prelude, she began shouting the whole story of Jane at him.

She had not realized it was such a long story. But, starting with the egg, she brought him up to date, including the fact that Dick Fuller and the hunters were probably on the way to Loony Lake *right now!*

Mr. Grant listened calmly. He was hard to surprise, these days. At last she ran out of breath. He hit the sheet metal with the hammer, thoughtfully.

"I see," he said. "It's a little rough, isn't it, Gussie, to slap a man with a monster story in broad daylight? Why don't you save that for bedtime?"

Tex said quickly: "It's true though, Mr. Grant! There *is* a, well—a *beast* of some kind over there. It *did* hatch from an egg—an orange one."

Mr. Grant tapped a nail. "An orange one. Good! If it were white, I might have believed it."

"And it thinks Gussie's her mother—!"

"Impossible," said Gussie's father. "She isn't even married."

"Just shows to go you," Percy said sadly, "that it's best not to have secrets. Because there is a critter over there, Tom. I've seen it. I didn't tell you before, because I was afraid I was imagining it. Thought if I didn't pay any attention it might go away. And the kids were afraid you'd kill it. But I reckon it's there. And now it seems like Tex's father is coming up here to kill it."

Mr. Grant climbed down the ladder. "Percy, haven't you got some better news than this for a poor, tired rancher?"

"Why, yes, I have!" Percy said, brightly. "The lawyer just called and said the trees we cut do belong to you! The land we cut them on belonged to Andrews' father fifty, sixty years ago, but Fred used the strip on this side of the creek for at least fifty years—even fenced it in. And if you fence in a piece of land like that and use it forever, why, it becomes yours. My lawyer talked to Andrews' lawyer, and it's all settled. They've got no case, and you can keep the money *and* the land!"

Gussie was glad to hear it. But that didn't help to solve the problem of Jane. And hearing them begin to talk about it, she knew that they were *afraid* of the Jane story! That they were quite happy to forget about it. As Percy had said, if you'd lived in a non-monster world too long, it was hard to believe in them. So, she knew, she would have to do something to make them believe in it.

She turned away. "Okay, Daddy," she said. "I'm going back there myself and stop them! And they'll all have guns. It'll be your fault if—"

Mr. Grant caught her under his arm. "Nobody's going to shoot anything on our land without permission," he sighed. "Not even a monster."

Tex rode in Percy's truck, and Gussie rode with her father. They drove up the steep road from the pasture. "You say Dr. Wigmore saw the animal?" Mr. Grant said.

Gussie chewed anxiously on one of her braids. It was important, she knew, not to frighten him with words like "dinosaur."

"Yes. She said it's *like* some animal that I've forgotten the name of. But this animal's been dead for, well, a hundred million years or so, so Jane—"

"So Jane isn't a dinosaur?"

She was amazed at how quickly he picked up on things. Also, she saw something like a happy smile playing on his lips.

"Not *exactly*, but—"

"But pretty close."

"Yes. Pretty close, I guess."

"I'll tell you what. I'm going to call Dr. Wigmore from the house, on the way over. I want to find out all I can about this animal in the shortest space of time. Personally, I see no reason why we couldn't call it a dinosaur. The *last* dinosaur, maybe. The last dinosaur. . . !"

22

DR. WIGMORE must have convinced him that Jane was a real dinosaur, because he came from the house shaking his arms in the air.

"A dinosaur!" he shouted. "Would you believe that? *A real duck-billed dinosaur!* Come on—I want to see this lake monster of yours!"

He picked up a rock and threw it as far as he could, then climbed into Percy's truck. The children scrambled in back, behind the cab, and Gussie could hear him yelling things at Percy as they headed up the road to the highway.

But just as they reached Old 101, two cars came along the road. The car in the lead was the hunters' blue pickup. The other car was Mr. Fuller's. They passed in a snarl of sound, and Percy took off after them. The wind made the children's eyes water as he sped to catch up.

They reached the other cars at the gate. One of the hunters held a pair of bolt cutters and was preparing to cut the chain. Gussie's father jumped out and ran up to him.

"Oh no you don't!" he said. "That's my property, friend."

Dick Fuller stepped forward with a rifle in his hands. "Man-killers are public property, Mr. Grant," he said. "I'm taking over here."

Mr. Grant laughed. "Really? You're going to trespass on my land—at gunpoint? Why, Dick, I'm surprised at you. They'd put you in prison for that. You should know that."

Gussie saw at once that Dick Fuller did know it. Because he licked his lips in frustration, looked at the other men, and lowered his gun.

"Sure," he said, trying to smile. He was panting with excitement. "I didn't mean that we were going to break in, Mr. Grant. I'm just counting on you to show good sense and invite us in—"

"I'll invite the sheriff in, if he comes with a warrant," said Mr. Grant.

The hunter called Otey shook the gate with both hands. "Grant, there's a dangerous beast down there! It killed your wife's uncle. And if it isn't put to death, there'll be more killing. Use your head, man—"

"Apparently I'm the only one who is. That animal is too small to kill anything. Plus, there is no proof that

Fred Hill was killed by anything but a tractor. But I agree that it's time a study was made of the animal."

With a snarl of vexation, Otey started back to his truck. "Come on, men! We can get the sheriff and be back in an hour."

Gussie was proud of her father. She threw her arms around him and said: "You were great, Daddy! What will you do when they come back?"

Mr. Grant frowned as he sorted through a large bunch of keys. "I'm sorry you asked that," he said. "Because I don't know. I've got to slow them down before they can hurt that animal. I suppose you know the sheriff pretty well, don't you, Percy?"

Percy glanced guiltily at the air to his left. "Why, I guess you could say so. Yes, I know him. . . ."

"I gather," Gussie's father said uneasily, "that he knows you too?"

"I ran for office against Sheriff Butts last year," Percy admitted. "He's been sheriff for twenty years, and I thought he needed competition. He's too fat and lazy for a lawman. I only got sixteen votes—it was more of a joke—but he's never forgiven me."

"Great," groaned Mr. Grant. "He'll be a lot of help. I can see that."

As they drove down to the lake, Gussie tried to decide how to handle the introduction of Jane to her father. It was important not to frighten him. She wished Jane were pretty and cuddly, like a kitten, for if she came charging up to him looking for a snack, she might scare him up a tree.

Percy parked near the fir woods and Gussie jumped from the truck and ran ahead. "I'll find her!" she cried. "When you hear me blow the horn, you can come on."

She found Jane standing in the mud at the lake's edge, near a bush in which Gussie had hidden her French horn. Mud and vines draped her to her shoulders, as she browsed contentedly on wild rice. Seeing Gussie, Jane came wading toward her with little yelps of affection. Gussie offered her some water-lily leaves, although the animal was perfectly capable, now, of handling all her feeding problems. But Jane still liked to be babied.

Suddenly there was a shout from the edge of the woods.

"Gussie! Get back! That thing might—"

It was her father. He and the others had followed. Jane regarded them in apprehension. Mr. Grant picked up a fallen branch, as a club, and Jane snorted with delight and frolicked toward him. She thought it was something to eat, Gussie realized. And she had learned that anyone who came with her was friendly, so she had no fear.

Mr. Grant backed up, the club raised.

"She won't hurt you!" Gussie screamed. "Drop the branch."

Jane's jaws closed on the club, and she tugged until Mr. Grant let go of it. She tried eating it, but after a moment dropped it in disappointment. After nosing it, she began sniffing Mr. Grant to see what else he might have brought her. Gussie's father stood frozen while the gray-green duckbill plucked at his clothing.

Gussie ran over, tugging at Jane until she moved away a couple of feet.

"Pick some ferns and give them to her! She just wants to eat." Then she remembered what Dr. Wigmore had said of the Camptosaurus. "She's a gentle beast. She won't hurt you."

Gussie demonstrated how the Camptosaurus would play dead, submerge, and come at her call. "Isn't she smart?" she said. Jane swam for them and waddled up and down the beach. Slowly Gussie's father conquered his fear of the animal. He reached out to stroke her cold, wet hide. Then he examined her teeth and her feet, and finally fed her some leaves. At last he leaned against a tree, smiling to himself, and watched Gussie and Tex feed her. He seemed in a trance.

All at once Percy, who was mournfully chewing on a blade of grass, raised his head and seemed to listen to something. "Car coming!" he warned.

They all listened. In the evening stillness, over the crunch of ferns in Jane's bill, the hum of an auto came like the drone of angry bees. Then the cry of a siren rose like a sudden scream. A moment later, Gussie saw a black-and-white car arrive at the gate. Four men piled out of it. While one of them cut the chain, a fat man in a tan uniform scanned the lake with binoculars.

Gussie clutched her father's arm. "Daddy? What are you going to tell the sheriff?"

Everything—the whole future of dinosaurs on earth —would depend on his convincing the men, before they could shoot Jane, that she was harmless!

Suddenly Percy said angrily: "One of those idiots is pointing a gun this way!"

An instant later something struck the water near Jane with a loud *ploop!* Spray spurted upward, and the little lake creature raised her head, startled. Then the splitting crash of a rifle shot poured down the hill.

Gussie ran to where she had left the horn.

23

"THOSE IDIOTS! Those morons!" yelled Mr. Grant. "Where can we hide her?"

Gussie was already filling her lungs to blow the distress call. The Camptosaurus pulled up a clump of water lilies with a sucking sound, unperturbed. But as the strong, urgent cry of Taps split the air, she turned, waded into deeper water, and paddled frantically into the lake. Another shot hit the water near her. A few moments later, Jane sank in a ring of ripples.

But how long could she stay underwater? Gussie wondered.

The sheriff's car passed through the gate and came lunging down the road. It passed out of sight behind the trees. A couple of minutes later, up to its axles in mud, it lunged through an elderberry thicket and came to a halt on the beach. A very small rowboat was lashed to a rack on its top.

Dick Fuller and the hunters scrambled from the car, followed by a fat man in a tan uniform. Sheriff Butts filled his uniform the way a wiener fills its skin. He carried a shotgun, and a revolver was holstered on his hip. As if on cue, the men formed themselves into a sort of ring, like wagon trains braced for an Indian attack.

"Where is it?" shouted Sheriff Butts. "Percy, get these people out of the way! There's going to be shooting—"

Gussie ran at him, screeching: "Don't touch her! She's a gentle beast!"

But her father tucked Gussie under his arm and told the sheriff: "Put your firearms down, sheriff. The only danger anyone is in is from you. I've examined the animal, and it's perfectly harmless."

"Harmless! You should have seen Fred Hill after he was trampled to death. Get back, now—"

Mr. Grant set Gussie down and began trying to wrest the gun from the sheriff's hands. Immediately Dick Fuller and the hunters dropped their own weapons and tackled Gussie's father. Gussie ran back to her horn, picked it up, and blew Taps, to make sure Jane did not start coming ashore. Tex ran up and began arguing with his father. Percy stood near the police car shaking his head.

All the men except the sheriff were down in a heap now, trying to subdue Mr. Grant. He was shouting the strangest things.

"Best thing that ever happened to your economy, and you want to kill it! Perfectly harmless. Even my little daughter— *Get your knee out of my back!*"

They dragged him to a small tree, wrapped his arms around its trunk, and the sheriff handcuffed his wrists together. Mr. Grant was still yelling at them about the economy, and a bigger and better Agate City, but no one was listening. The sheriff bawled:

"The critter must be still in the lake! Get that boat in the water—"

While they unloaded the small duck-hunting boat, Gussie held her father's handcuffed hands. "Are you all right, Daddy?"

Her father had stopped straining, but he was red and angry. "Yes, but keep on blowing your horn. Horns helped at Jericho. They may help here."

Dick Fuller and the sheriff carried the little boat to the edge of the water. It looked barely large enough for two men, but all four seemed bent on taking part in the hunt. Three of them crowded in and sat down with their rifles. Fuller pushed the boat into deeper water, then climbed in, his pants and shoes black and dripping. The sheriff pulled strongly on the oars, pausing once to yell:

"Stop that fool horn-blowing! I can't even think with all that racket."

Mr. Grant turned his head to shout back at him: "You

126

couldn't think in the quiet room of the public library, Butts! You're trying to kill the greatest thing that's ever happened to Agate City!"

The boat went zigzagging out onto the lake. Every time a man pointed his arm at this or that, the little craft tilted. The men were packed into it like chickens in a crate.

Tex tugged at Gussie's arm. "Jane's going to suffocate if she stays under too long!"

Gasping for breath, Gussie said: "So am I! But if she comes up, they'll shoot her." She started blowing again.

"They're right where she submerged now," Tex said. "Man, look at the boat rock—! And my dad can't swim, even after twenty years in the Navy."

Gussie stopped blowing to get her breath. Red-faced, she told Tex: "Then he ought to know better than to go out in a little boat like that."

She panted a while, studying the lake. Nothing broke its dark surface but the ripples created by the boat. Gussie was so winded that she could hardly think. In fact, when she put the mouthpiece to her lips to resume blowing Taps, she had to stop and review the first few notes. She remembered, and blew the call with desperate force.

Then she saw Tex shudder. He yanked the horn from her lips. "That's the wrong tune! If she hears that, she'll surface!"

Gussie wailed in fright. In her excitement, she had

played the all-clear signal! She gasped another breath and tried to blow Taps, but the sounds came out in a broken sputter.

Out on the lake, the sheriff grasped the sides of the rowboat and yelled: "Whichever one of you is rocking this boat had better—"

"Sit still!" bawled Dick Fuller, in panic. "You're going to spill us!"

The strange thing was, Gussie saw, the boat was rocking crazily—but no one in it was moving! They were sitting very still. So something else had to be rocking it.

Suddenly it heeled to one side. The men all slid that way, shouting. The boat hesitated an instant, then rolled over. The men disappeared beneath the surface.

A few feet away, Jane's head broke into view. It was she who had tipped the boat over by surfacing under it. She gazed in astonishment at the men who came bobbing to the surface. They threshed about the little boat. All of them had let go their rifles as the boat capsized. And now three of them, panicked by Jane, struck out for shore.

Mr. Grant was laughing. But over his laughter came a shout from Mr. Fuller.

"I can't swim!"

The other men did not look back. They were interested only in escaping from the man-eating lake monster who was cruising around Dick Fuller, nuzzling him. Mr. Fuller would paddle wildly, sink, then surface to take a breath and paddle again.

Tex pulled off his shoes. "I'll try to save him," he gasped. "I got a lifesaving pin last summer, but he's pretty big—"

Then Gussie saw Jane put her bill into Dick Fuller's face and make a honking noise at him, as if trying to get him to play with her. In terror of drowning, he suddenly wrapped his arms around the animal's neck. Jane began swimming in a circle, thinking Mr. Fuller wanted to play. She held her head high and honked in delight.

Gussie grinned when she realized how to save Mr. Fuller. He would hate it!

Filling her lungs, she began blowing the all-clear tune. Jane obediently turned toward shore. With Mr. Fuller clinging to her neck, the monster swam toward Gussie. Mr. Fuller finally lost his hold, but by that time he was in water only two feet deep.

Gussie met Jane at the edge of the water. "Good girl," she said. She laid down the horn and pulled up some water plants. At the edge of the woods, she saw Sheriff Butts and the hunters watching her. One of the hunters had climbed a small tree. Dick Fuller, exhausted, remained doglike on hands and knees in six inches of water.

Gussie fed Jane the leaves, then stroked her cold, wet head. Then she had her open her mouth, and put her hand inside to show that she would not bite. Turning her head, she called to the sheriff:

"See? She's a gentle beast, just like Dr. Wigmore says. It's all right now. Don't you want to feed her something?"

24

LONG AFTER the other men had accepted hot coffee and dry clothes and driven from the ranch house, Mr. Fuller sat shivering before the big fire Percy had built. In the kitchen, Gussie's mother was frying pork chops. In the parlor, Gussie knelt beside her father, who was telephoning the editor of the Agate City newspaper.

". . . So naturally I want the local paper to be the one to break the news. A live dinosaur—I kid you not! But let's get one fact straight, and Sheriff Butts will verify it: The animal is perfectly harmless. In fact, it saved the life of Dick Fuller. Right, Dick?" he called.

Mr. Fuller had had two cans of beer and was now drinking coffee, huddled before the flames in Mr. Grant's white terry-cloth robe. "Affirmative on that, Tom!" he responded.

". . . She's a plant-eater, not a meat-eater. Call Jane Wigmore for the facts. Now, here's where you come in. We're going to have armies of people swarming around here wanting to see the 'lake monster.' I'd like you to emphasize in your stories that the animal is absolutely harmless—that my daughter and I, as well as Dick and the sheriff, have all fed her by hand."

Gussie brought another cup of coffee to her father and resumed her seat on the rug.

"We're applying to the National Science Foundation for a grant to take care of the animal. Dr. Wigmore will be in charge. Eventually, the Park Service may want to buy the land. All we know for sure is that every business firm in Agate City will be swamped trying to take care of visitors. It will be a Gold Rush! So it will be important to all of us to see that Jane is protected—that shots aren't fired at her and people don't try to feed her popcorn, broken glass, and tin cans. I've asked the National Guard to take over until we get things under control here."

Mr. Grant ended his call and Gussie helped her mother serve dinner at the big kitchen table. But she poked at her food, feeling unhappy. In a way, she was more worried about Jane than she had been before. Busloads of people would be coming to gawk at Jane and hear somebody lecture. Naturally they wouldn't pay any attention to a nine-year-old girl with a French horn.

Gussie's mother squeezed her hand and whispered to her: "I'm so proud of you!"

Gussie shrugged.

Dick Fuller reached over to tap Tex's arm with his fork. Tex had not been eating much, either. "Eat up there, skipper," he growled. "You won't get chow like this after you come home."

"You're telling me," Tex muttered. "Frozen pizza three times a day. Yecch."

Gussie spoke up. "Why can't Tex stay with us this summer? We still need a hired man, and I guess we'll have enough money to pay him, now."

Mr. Grant chortled. "You'd better believe it!"

Fuller stifled a belch. "Well, as far as I'm concerned, it'd be fine. But I don't know if your folks would want another kid around, Gus."

"Certainly we would," Gussie's mother said. "Tex is a fine boy."

"We could keep him busy all summer," said Percy, sneaking a pork-chop bone down to Al, at his side. Al began to chew it with a sound like splintering wood.

Mr. Fuller gazed at Tex, then at the Grants. Finally he asked, puzzled: "Does he really behave himself out here?"

"Of course!" Mrs. Grant laughed. "What is he, Dick, some kind of delinquent?"

"Maybe I'm not much of a hand with kids. But the way I always looked at it, you could train kids just like you train recruits in the Navy. When I said frog, those trainees of mine jumped! I busted many a man for not making his bunk like I told him, or having a shirt pocket unbuttoned. They hated me at the time, but after we'd been in battle and come through with honors, they thanked me."

He looked around, as if for applause. Tex kept his head down and ate steadily. The other adults looked embarrassed, Gussie thought.

"But I don't know," Fuller said doubtfully. "Tex don't act happy, like he should. He's not a bad kid, so maybe it's me. Maybe I haven't been much of a father. And I shouldn't have gone off half-cocked, like I did today. I'm sorry about that."

Percy sipped some coffee, then asked cheerfully: "Ever thought of going back to sea, Dick?"

"Does a fat man ever think of hot fudge sundaes? Every night, bar none, I look over my old Navy scrapbook! All my promotions—my decorations—my favorite liberty ports. If it weren't for the kid, I'd re-enlist tomorrow."

Gussie saw Tex stop chewing. She knew he must feel terrible! And she looked at her mother and saw her wince, as though she had stuck a needle in her finger.

Percy took another pork chop from the platter, passed another bone down to Al, who was crashing away steadily on the last one, and said:

"If I felt that way, Dick, I'd put Tex in a foster home or some such and re-enlist. Maybe the Grants would board him. Unless he goes wild and forgets to button his shirt pocket or something. What about it, Fern? Think you could handle a rotten kid like Tex?"

Mrs. Grant put her arm around Tex and gave him a squeeze. "Oh, I think so. As long as he jumped every time I said frog. What about it, Tex?"

Tex glared around the table, but shrugged and grinned and passed his hand over his hair. "Don't matter to me. Suit yourselves. Hey, Grant, how'd you like Sheriff Butts in your father's jeans? He couldn't button the top four buttons!"

They laughed about it. Gussie was pleased, but still worried about Jane. She could just see some famous animal trainer coming in and taking over with Jane. Jane would become just like Tex—motherless and hard to handle. And for all they knew, unhappy lake monsters probably died of sorrow in a short time.

"So what do you want to do about Jane?" her father was asking her.

Gussie looked up. "I thought you were going to give her to the National Science Foundation or something."

Her father shook his head. "She's yours. She'll have to be protected, but we won't make any big moves without consulting you. Where do we start?"

"With a fence," Gussie said promptly. "Her mother probably learned to stay out of sight, because she was born before there were people here. That's what Dr. Wigmore thinks. So she got used to them and learned she'd better stay in the woods or underwater most of the time. But Jane will want to wander all over, so we'll need a big fence. Can we afford one?"

"Absolutely! The whole idea is to let her develop naturally."

Gussie frowned. "I hope she won't be like a sideshow freak. You know how people are."

"The way I see it, the entire Loony Lake area will have to be kept exactly as it is. It's her natural environment. We'll build a shelter of some kind where people can watch her without being seen. Of course we'll have to let a few scientists examine Jane now and then, and you can show them around."

Gussie had a vision of herself strolling along the lake's edge while people watched from the woods. She would blow the all-clear signal on her horn. Jane would trumpet back to her and swim from the deep water to the shore, where Gussie would give her a water-lily blossom to eat. By this time Jane would be eight feet high—as big as an elephant!

Scientists would stand by respectfully, asking questions.

"Have you noticed whether water lilies give her more energy than ferns? How did you teach her which signal means danger, and which means to come to you? How long can she stay underwater? Do you think her parents may still be living down there, coming out at night?

Gussie would say, "No, Dr. Wigmore and I think her mother and father probably moved. As far as Jane is concerned, I'm her mother now."

And Jane would come up, honking and splashing, and nuzzle her for a fern frond.

FRANK BONHAM is widely acclaimed as a children's book author. His well-known inner-city dramas are set in Dogtown, a fictionalized West Coast ghetto. For *The Friends of the Loony Lake Monster*, Mr. Bonham has drawn on his experiences in southwest Oregon. He says of the story: "The legend about the buried treasure is said to be true, but I haven't found anything but old bottles yet." Mr. Bonham also has a friend in Oregon who raises sheep. "I have helped him herd sheep, repair fence, and haul a tractor." Mr. Bonham and his family live in La Jolla, California.